DEFENDER OF MAGIC

DEFENDER OF MAGIC

THE LEIRA CHRONICLES™ BOOK 9

MARTHA CARR

MICHAEL ANDERLE

DISRUPTIVE IMAGINATION

LMBPN Publishing
PMB 196, 2540 South Maryland Pkwy
Las Vegas, NV 89109

First US Edition August 2020
Version 1.01, October 2020
eBook ISBN: 978-1-64971-097-0
Print ISBN: 978-1-64971-098-7

Thank you to Early Readers
Debi Sateren and Kathleen Fettig
If I've missed anyone, please let me know!

From Martha

To everyone who still believes in magic and all the possibilities that holds.

To all the readers who make this entire ride so much fun.

To Louie, Jackie, and so many wonderful friends who remind me all the time of what really matters and how wonderful life can be in any given moment.

And finally, a special thank you to John Nelson of the Austin, Texas Police Department who patiently answers all of my questions. I hope I made you proud. Thank you for your service.

From Michael

To Family, Friends and
Those Who Love
To Read.
May We All Enjoy Grace
To Live The Life We Are
Called.

CHAPTER ONE

The loud ring of Leira's cell phone broke through her deep sleep. She groaned, rolled over in the bed and slapped at the nightstand. Correk stirred in his sleep and swatted at the air. "Yumfuck, those are mine," he muttered, his face pressed into the pillow. Leira gave a crooked smile and put one hand on his back, brushing aside his long hair. She pulled the phone toward her face and squinted at the bright light from the screen.

Blocked number. Her heart rate picked up, hoping it was one of her new contacts.

It was taking some effort to cultivate the hidden eyes and ears in Washington DC. Turner Underwood was helping with the start of a network among the magicals and there was some progress. Still, no one was giving up Wolfstan Humphrey. *Well, almost no one.*

The Dark Families were easier. There were more disgruntled witches and wizards willing to talk for a price. Family, go figure.

I went out on my own to hunt these motherfuckers. Still takes a village... just a slightly darker one.

Leira sat up and swung her legs over the edge of the bed, kicking a moving box with her toe. "Fuck me!" she hissed, swallowing the rest of it. She glanced back at Correk and got up, weaving around the boxes to get out of the bedroom and down the hall.

"For the love of..." Her foot recoiled from a piece of broken stone in the unfinished part of her new house. *Their* new house.

"Hello?"

"You're coming in hot. Everything okay?" General Anderson barked into the phone.

Leira swallowed, balancing on one foot and leaning against the kitchen counter. "Yeah, just stumbling around in the dark. Hit a few domestic land mines."

"I have a tip for you that should make you feel better. I know you don't work for me anymore, but this one is going to take your unique skill set."

"One that can't wait until the sun comes up?"

"No... Good info never lasts long, you know that. I got it from an old contact of mine who operates off the grid."

"You mean a felon."

"No, he's never been caught. If we only gather intel from vetted sources, we'll always be a few yards behind. I want to get ahead. I'm sending you the coordinates. A powerful artifact was left behind by an old wizard who jumped back to Oriceran. You might be able to get it before word spreads."

"Okay," she yawned. "I'm on it."

"Best of luck. Stay in touch. You can use this number. It's analog and untraceable."

"Will we need to chat that often?"

"I have a feeling we will need each other more than we can imagine right now."

The general hung up without another word. His usual sign off. Leira hung up and took a deep breath. There was never a bad time to get a powerful artifact out of reach of darker sources, especially with Wolfstan Humphrey out there. She tiptoed back into the room and kissed Correk on the forehead, grabbing her pants, a UT t-shirt, and boots from the table and headed to the bathroom to get dressed.

She saw the tiny troll's green hair poking out of the top drawer of her dresser. He was neatly tucked in a pair of pale blue panties and was snoring softly. Her constant companion bonded to her for life. Yumfuck Tiberius Troll, formerly of Oriceran.

"Should I take you?" she whispered, rubbing the top of his head. He trilled and curled into a ball. "Nah, it's early. And this one should be a grab and go."

It was about time something was simple. She finished getting ready in the one bathroom in the Georgian row house, pulling a brush through her dark hair and heading down two flights to the empty living room on the first floor.

She caught sight of something shiny and orange poking out from under the couch and leaned down closer in the darkness to get a better look. Underneath were piles of empty Cheetos bags. "Oh Yumfuck, you've been gaslighting Correk and sneaking his stash. This will come back to bite you, my little furry friend." She pushed the trash further back. "An argument for another day."

Leira looked down at the coordinates on her phone. *London. Nice change of pace.*

The Jasper Elf closed her eyes and drew energy from the ground, up through her body. "Almost as good as coffee." Symbols flashed across her skin, changing at a rapid pace. She held up an arm and read the first few lines. "Damn, there's already a few lookey loos." She formed a ball of light in her hands, pulling it apart and whispering into it the coordinates.

Sunlight streamed into the living room, making Leira blink as her eyes adjusted. "My own kind of jet lag." On the other side was a narrow alley behind a cluster of three-story buildings. "How does he manage to get coordinates to an alley?" She pulled her jacket closer against the damp air, the portal closing with a snap and a fizz, sparks dancing across the blacktop.

"You're a bit late."

Leira startled, putting her hands up, ready to fight, as a Light Elf leaned out of the shadows, dressed in a windbreaker and jeans. "I was expecting you an hour ago. I thought you Federal types were punctual."

"Who the hell are you?"

The Elf circled her, sizing her up. "Didn't your general tell you? He's a cagey one. I guess he figured we'd sort it out. I'm a Light Elf, born here in Clapham and stayed here all my life. My name's Daniel and, no, there's no last name."

"You're a little short for a Light Elf."

"Not a good way to start a relationship, dearie. I have

feelings, you know. Come on, the sun's already up. We don't have a lot of time."

"I'm Leira."

"I know... I've heard of you."

"You're the source, I take it."

"I am. The general and me, we go way back. He saved my ass a few times and I owe him." He gave Leira the side eye as they came out onto the street. "You're that Jasper Elf everyone's talking about, aren't you?"

"Does it matter?"

"I suppose not. Come on, we're meeting in the park. A Dwarf got his hands on the artifact and it hasn't turned out well for him. He wants it gone."

"What does that mean?"

"You'll see. Bit of an issue."

They walked swiftly across the park, avoiding the path of a few runners and made their way to a bandstand topped by a blue ornamental dome supported by thin iron pillars.

"Empty. Damn. He must have gotten spooked. Not your lucky day. I don't see him anywhere."

"Give me a minute." Leira took a deep breath and set an intention. The magic took over, sending out an orb of light that shot up into the sky and moved across the landscape. It was searching for the hum of an artifact, absorbing traces of nearby magic.

Where are you? Aha! There you are. Quite a bit of dark magic in you.

"Gobshite!" Daniel looked up with his mouth wide open, watching the light bob and weave high in the trees, jumping over a trio of ponds, circling the entire two hundred and twenty acres.

Finally, it split in two, half of it turning back, zipping overhead and landing in Leira's hands, the glow shining under her chin.

"Who the hell taught you that neat trick? Can you teach me?"

"The Fixer and no." Leira smelled the piece of orb, a metallic residue lingering in her mouth There was a whiff of darkness in the orb, but not enough to put Leira on high alert.

"Well?" Daniel leaned closer, snorting in air. "I don't get it. Nothing."

"Your buddy is still here." Leira headed quietly across the trails, keeping to the edges just in case.

"I never said friend. More of a useful acquaintance." Daniel took to a stumbling trot, trying to keep up with Leira as she began to run, following the dissipating trail. It felt good to stretch her legs. *It's a run in a London park. This job's not all bad.*

She got to the edges of the tall sweet chestnut trees, running her hands along the moist bark for added grounding, just like Turner Underwood had taught her.

"There." The remnants of the orb, a tennis-ball-sized white ring of light, bobbed up and down at the top of the hill, across from an old church. A magical placeholder.

"Circle marks the spot," she whispered.

"Very clever."

She glanced up at the stately red brick church topped by a white steeple sitting on the edge of the park. The ring of light waited patiently just in front of it, moving in the shadows of trees fluttering in the chilly breeze. She walked toward the magical tracer, letting out a deep breath and concentrating on sensing the artifact's pull. As she got closer, she shook her head, wrinkling her forehead.

"Something's off." The metallic taste was getting stronger, but there was the trace of something else, crossing its path.

Zing!

A streak of blue light flashed overhead and struck the ring dead center, exploding it into a puff of smoke. Leira crouched down, pulling in magic as a wizard in a long navy blue woolen coat came down the stairs. Sirius.

"Fuck me. It's a trap."

"Now what? There's still a Dwarf somewhere clutching an artifact. He is having the worst day ever. Damn wizards. They ruin it for everybody." Daniel crouched down next to her, lighting a fireball in his palm. "What? You didn't think I was gonna run, did you? Bollocks. I'm a little hardier than that."

Sirius smiled menacingly at Leira, tapping his crooked wand in his palm.

"Hello bitches."

"Well that hurt," said Daniel, pitching the fireball. Sirius flicked it away without taking his gaze off Leira. The wizard chuckled as he strode toward her, the hem of his coat dampening in the wet grass. "I didn't actually think this ploy would work. It must be the human in you."

"Looks like you bent your wand there, Sirius," Leira called out, ignoring the dig as she rolled a dark fireball in her hands, burning a brilliant orange in the center. "You lose to a Dwarf?" She held up the fireball and whispered, "Find your target."

The fiery ball of light whizzed straight at the wizard. Sirius swiped his wand through the air, leaning back, forcing it to curve to the right and circle, burning him along his back. He gritted his teeth in pain, muttering a spell and sent the remains of the fireball into one of the nearby ponds.

"I liked this coat," he said, breathing hard, his face flushed and still walking toward Leira and Daniel.

"What do we do? Should I try flanking him?" Daniel glanced over at a stand of red maples, judging the distance.

"You didn't think you could get my dear wife killed and not have to face consequences?"

"You created that scenario, Sirius when you decided to dabble in dark magic and shifters."

"Shifters? Shite." Daniel spit out the words.

"Get to the church. Your friend is in there. I'll follow as soon as I can."

"I like your optimism." Daniel took off at a run, crouching down and keeping an eye on Sirius. The wizard ignored him, closing in on Leira. She felt herself relax and she stood up, bracing herself for the attack, another dark fireball in her hand, burning at its core.

"You gave that Gnome the artifact, didn't you?"

Sirius shrugged, stopping a few yards from her. "It was an old family heirloom gathering dust in a vault. Too dangerous to be used, really. Till today."

"Let's do this." Leira centered her mind and sent out an intention. *Take his power.* The energy coursed through her body and glowed from her eyes and her fingertips. She looked down at the symbols on her arms flipping over furiously, showing possible outcomes of the fight.

They were moving so fast she could barely make them out, but one caught her attention and she wrinkled her nose, perplexed. *Shifters? What do they have to do with this?*

The light left her hands just as Sirius flicked his wand, weaving a cloud of blue powder that formed into a spear heading straight at Leira.

The energies collided, pushing back and forth, edging closer to Leira. She growled in irritation, counted to three and dropped to the ground, letting the spray of magic shoot over her head. She rolled to the side and hurled another fireball, watching it split into four, circling the wizard.

Sirius swiped away all but one. The burning magical ember hit him in the shoulder, singeing through his wool coat and burning his flesh. He screamed in pain and anger and sent fireballs back at her, shaking the embers off his clothes as she neatly dodged them.

"I should have brought the troll." She bit her lip and stood back up with her hands on her hips, setting a new intention. "Fuck second thoughts. Today's not your day, Sirius."

The energy rolled quickly along the ground in front of her, seeking out Sirius, making the bracelet on her wrist rattle as it worked at grounding her. Heat radiated through her body and the scar on her belly ached.

Sirius raised his wand and braced himself against the light. "Defendendum lucem!" His feet dug into the grass, the energy pushing him backward toward the church steps.

"You should have brought your minions," Leira growled, feeling the energy push harder against her bracelet.

Sirius bellowed in anger, the sound cutting through the whine of the energy coursing through her. He was barely visible through the glare of the white light, but she pushed harder, determined to strip him of his magic. "I can do this." She bit off the words, gritting her teeth.

A crimson red flare burst, splintering and digging holes through the white light. The shards of dark energy came at her, too fast to dodge and hitting her square in the chest.

Leira sucked in air, disconnecting her connection to the magic as she was thrown backward. She landed on her back, grabbing her chest, the flare sizzling in small red dots against her skin.

A fireball exploded next to her face, and she winced as she pulled herself into a crouch.

"No one's coming to help you, Leira." Sirius smiled, raising his broken wand. "We are finally at the end of this story."

Leira pulled herself to her knees, pushing off the ground, determined to face Sirius on her feet. Sparks showered around her, a portal tearing open next to her. Correk stepped through, his longbow already armed and Yumfuck leaping off his shoulder.

"You were saying?" Leira steadied herself, ignoring any pain.

The troll grew to eight feet tall, advancing on Sirius, roaring as he swiped through the air with his claws. Correk lit the end of the arrow with a fireball, letting it fly toward its target and piercing Sirius' shoulder.

"That one was for Alan, asshole. And it's just the first of many," growled Leira.

Sirius cried out in pain, encircling himself with his wand. "Obumbratio!" Shadows rose up suddenly around him, evaporating along with the injured wizard.

"What the hell? How did he do that?" Leira gingerly touched the side of her face and all the nicks the flare had left behind in her skin.

"Dark magic has a lot of ways." Correk tied the longbow on his back and gently wrapped his arms around Leira.

"I'm okay. That was close." She turned her head at the few people in the park, running toward them. "We have company."

Correk let go of her and held up his hand. "Never was, never will be."

The humans froze where they were as the spell spread throughout the park.

"Do we leave them like that, or do we give them all smiles. I don't know."

Yumfuck shrunk back down to his five inch stature as Leira bent over and held out her hand. She lifted him up to her shoulder and stretched her back. "How did you know I needed you? Did the little guy turn blue? I wasn't in that deep."

"No, I'm the Fixer," he said, patting his chest. "You're a magical. You set off alarms."

Leira's eyes grew wider. "Wow... I never got how much you're like a superhero till just now. You need a cape like Batfuck here."

"Good, you're making jokes. Nothing broken."

"No, but there's a Dwarf who may need more

assistance. Come on, I say we leave the humans and let them wonder why they're running. We need to get out of sight before that spell wears off."

Correk arched an eyebrow but followed her toward the church. "How did you end up here in the first place?"

"Tip from General Anderson. The Dark Families managed to fool him, which means there's a mole in his operation. Not good news."

Leira took the steps two at a time, ignoring the ache in her bones. The metallic taste returned, and she followed the trail inside the darkened church and down the center aisle, careful not to step on the red carpet runner down the middle.

They found Daniel in the chancel behind the altar, a Dwarf cowering behind him, clutching a duffel bag to his chest.

"You lived!" Daniel broke into a wide grin. "And you brought backup. Marvelous. We'll need it." He stepped aside to reveal the Dwarf. "Stand up, Fitz. Show 'em what you've done to yourself. He played with the damn thing."

Fitz sheepishly stood up, stretching to seven feet, his torso much longer than his legs.

"Oh..." Leira hesitated, her brow furrowed. "The artifact... did that?"

"Yeah, go on, Fitz. Tell them. He was a bit of a minger before, but he's gone and made it even worse."

"Fuck off, Daniel. You're not so easy on the eyes either," whined Fitz. "The wizard said it would grant me a wish. I paid him ten quid for it. It should have worked."

"It kind of did," said Leira. "Is the artifact in the bag?" She held out her hand and Fitz reluctantly handed it over.

Inside was a bowl made of pink quartz. "Probably not a good idea to try to fix him with this thing."

"You would be right," said Correk, crossing his arms over his chest.

"Do you have something else? I've got nothing."

A shudder passed through Fitz, his bottom lip trembling. "There, there, Fitz. The Fixer is here," said Daniel. "Yeah, I know who you are. Word travels pretty fast when the baton is passed, so to speak. Nice to meet you. I'm Daniel... No last name. I don't like using them."

"So you said," said Leira. "Fitz, how did you get that artifact?"

"On the dark web. There's a channel just for magicals where you can find anything. I saw a notice on a bulletin board in a chat room."

"A virtual Dark Market. I wonder if Harkin can help us get on it."

Correk grimaced. "I wouldn't be surprised to find out he helped create it. Are you ready?" Correk reached up and put his hands on Fitz' shoulders.

"Just like that?" Fitz squeezed his eyes shut. "Yeah, sure. Okay, yeah. Just do it. I can't stay like this."

"Fuckin A. I can't believe I actually get to see you at work," muttered Leira. "Okay, I'll be quiet." She held a finger up to her lips and the troll on her shoulder did the same, letting out a cackle.

Correk rolled his eyes but went back to focusing on Fitz. He pressed down on his shoulders, his hands glowing around the edges. "Cinis cinerem, pulvis et cinis. Reditum parit."

Fitz's mouth popped open and his eyes widened in

surprise. His bones creaked loudly, and his face twisted in pain as Correk continued to press down on his shoulders. "I change my mind!" screamed Fitz, but it was too late to go back. His muscles and bones reshaped themselves as Daniel leaned away, squeezing one eye shut, the other staring at the metamorphosis.

Finally, standing before them was a five foot Dwarf covered in sweat, his clothes hanging off him.

"I gotta say, Fitz. Now that I've seen the options, you're not bad looking like this," said Daniel.

"One last question, Fitz," said Leira. "Did the wizard give you this artifact personally?"

"Wizard?" Fitz wiped his forehead on his sleeve. "What are you talking about? I didn't get that bowl from a wizard. It was a Light Elf, like you," he said, nodding at Correk. "He said his name was Wolfstan Humphrey."

Leira felt her heart beat faster. "Sirius lied. He's the pawn in this whole thing, not the leader."

"He said someone would show up when the time was right to pick up the bowl and I was to tell them he said hello. I suppose that's you two."

Leira leaned back in a wide stance, her hands on her hips. "Wolfstan's fucking with us for his own pleasure. Fine. That's the way you make mistakes. His first one was using the general. Somewhere in that is a flaw and I'm going to find it. His second one was using the web. That thing leaves a trail better than magic." She looked at Correk, not saying anything.

He worked his jaw but finally let out a sigh. "No, his first mistake was not asking Sirius what artifact he was going to use and handing it over to us. This bowl may hold some answers on how to help Peyton. We'll ask Harkin for help. He'll know how to use this thing and dig into the web."

"Look at that. Your dad is our secret weapon," said Leira, patting him on the back as the troll let out a low whistle and shrugged.

CHAPTER TWO

"**D**amn the heat," Leira muttered, tapping the thermostat with her finger. "I've already changed my shirt twice today." The metal bracelet with its inset stone jangled on her wrist as she brushed a strand of dark hair behind her ear and tapped again. *Nothing.* "It's not the heat, it's the fucking humidity."

"You're from Texas. This is East Coast heat. Junior heat." Correk chuckled and reached into a box of blueberry Pop Tarts, pulling out a silvery wrapped package and tearing it open with his teeth. His long, pale hair was tied back with a thin, leather cord.

"Those are better toasted."

"Takes too long."

"I'm surprised you didn't try a fireball on one of them." Leira noticed him look away and smiled. "You incinerated it, didn't you?"

"Not all of them. Yumfuck seemed to like them. Hey, did you move my Cheetos? Pack of individual bags."

"What? Nope. Didn't move them." *Not a lie.* Leira

reached for her mug of coffee and felt a twinge, lifting her shirt to check on the purple and blue bruise on her hip. "Say nothing. I earned this bruise fair and square."

Correk stopped chewing and looked at Leira, choosing his words carefully. "You went alone, and Sirius was waiting for you. Wolfstan has gotten to the Dark Families..."

Leira cut him off, slurping the hot coffee. "We got more pieces of a thousand piece puzzle of a blue sky with just a few clouds. It was a win." She stood in the half-finished hallway with her hands on her hips. "And we rescued Fitz and even wounded Sirius. He'll be out for a few days at least."

"That only leaves the government, a few hundred other dark wizards and witches, some shifters..."

"And Fleeker, last time I checked. I get it."

"Top of the list."

"Still going to do my part to keep it from becoming outright chaos." Leira turned the dial, drawing magic through her feet and swirled the energy around the thermostat, her eyes momentarily glowing. "This thing really *is* broken."

Correk bit into the Pop Tart and gave her a sidelong glance. "Please take the troll when you go out hunting for them again. It's a request, that's all."

"Said the Fixer."

"He was growling last night for no apparent reason. We both knew you were in trouble."

She walked over and hugged Correk from behind, ignoring the squeaks in the old pine floor. "Those things are better hot. From a toaster. We have one here somewhere in one of these boxes." She bit him softly on the ear, still rounded from the glamour he kept in place to hide in plain sight.

"I tried. The electricity sparked out in the kitchen again. The heat in here has left them reasonably warm."

"DC in the summer with no air conditioning. You know this city was built on a swamp. I can't take it..."

"You lived through Armageddon on the streets of Paris and are undone by the heat."

"Let me fix it. Chill this place down. I can set an intention..."

"We said we would keep the magic to a minimum. Keep a low profile, not leave energy trails for anyone to follow..."

"Where's a Crystal to hug when you need one?" Leira threw up her hands and went upstairs to their bedroom to stand in front of the large fan. The bedroom was the only completely renovated space in the red brick townhouse along N Street in Georgetown.

She pulled her sweaty DC 101 Rock Station t-shirt away from her body and lifted her hair off her neck as she looked at the overturned picture on the dresser. She picked it up and looked at the photo from the dinner in the kemana.

Almost a perfect day. They even managed to get back to dinner after Wolfstan pulled his dramatic exit. She wiped the dust off Harkin's face. *Still on the run. We'll fix that too.*

"Mom, you're the really brave one." She smiled at the picture of her mother and grandmother hugging her from either side, swallowing hard.

Correk came in and stood next to her in front of the

fan, a few long strands of silver hair clinging to the side of his damp face.

"You okay?"

"I didn't realize till we moved that I lived in a small radius of Austin almost my entire life. And our place before Nana disappeared was not far from Estelle's. It's how I knew her in the first place."

"This will feel like home eventually."

"I know. I've already found the good coffee places and there's Rock Creek Park. That place even has corners where Yumfuck can run wild without being seen. Still, it's not weird Austin."

"DC is weird for a whole new set of elected reasons."

"True. Are you ever sorry we turned down Turner's tricked-out mansion in Foggy Bottom?" she asked quietly.

"Only at night when the fan sputters and I run out of Cheetos to bribe Yumfuck to fan me."

Leira gently elbowed him. "That would be funnier if it wasn't true. We own this place. That's a better deal. It's like we're grownups."

Correk lifted Leira's chin and kissed her. "Turner understood. I think he was even proud of us. Did you know I kept a key?"

"Did you know he gave me one?"

"Doesn't seem as cool now."

"He said he wanted to make sure we had access to his gym and that arsenal of weapons. But who exactly would we be fighting with that armory? Not humans. I can't do that."

"Turner has always been good at seeing what may be coming next and preparing."

"That's disturbing. He showed me a couple and he has weapons I've never seen before. Lois called to see how we were doing. She said the Silver Griffins are having more and more trouble reigning in magicals."

"I know... I see it every day as the Fixer. Elves and Gnomes turning up missing or dead at the hands of dark magic. Turner understands even if he doesn't like it."

"Maybe I'll head over to the old mansion today."

"You're doing it for the air conditioning."

"Not denying it. He keeps that fridge stocked like he knows we're going to stop by."

"Because we do all the time."

"He even has frozen Snickers. He's not fighting fair. How are you doing taking over as the Fixer? That was abrupt the way Turner pulled back as soon as we got here."

"He's got other projects now. The open warfare in Paris really unnerved him. But he's been known to show up occasionally. Like he can hear me trying to figure out what spell to use." Correk ran his hand under Leira's shirt and up her back. "Turner keeps an eye out for you too, whether you know it or not."

Leira held up the bottom of her t-shirt, exposing the round scar on her belly as the breeze made her shirt billow. "I know he does. I run into his magic trail from time to time. It's like a fingerprint."

"We'll get this place fixed up in time. Our second place together."

Leira gave him a crooked smile. "We'll always have Estelle's. This place isn't that bad." She patted Correk on the shoulder. "We need to get going. Daylight's burning."

"I'll get changed. You're going to have to let go of the

fan."

"One more minute." She finally pulled herself away from the fan and walked down the hallway, past the kitchen that was still layered in dirt in some of the corners from years of neglect by the previous owners.

She went into the living room and lifted a frond on the lush potted fern, rubbing the small furry head of the five-inch troll napping in the cool dirt. "Yumfuck, wake up. There's food in it for you." She smoothed back his green hair and let go of the frond.

Correk came back downstairs dressed in jeans and a t-shirt and his cowboy boots. "This townhouse isn't bad and it's really not that old, not in Oriceran terms."

"That's because your magical buildings were built centuries ago, and magic is sturdier than mortar. This place was originally built in 1788, which makes it an historical artifact in the human world."

"That makes *me* an historical artifact in the human world." Flecks of frosting were sticking to the edges of Correk's lips.

Leira tilted her head and kissed him, licking the transferred frosting off her lip. She wrinkled her nose at the crumbs falling off the front of his shirt and reached out to wipe them away.

"I got this." Yumfuck came scurrying into the room and ran up Correk's pant leg to suck up the crumbs like a mini-vacuum cleaner. Leira sighed and shook her head.

"Let me get dressed and I will do something about this kitchen situation," she said. "We'll get some real food for breakfast, even though you already hit up Sam's Club without a place to cook anything."

Correk smiled. "You don't need to cook Doritos."

"Mmmm, Doritos," Yumfuck chimed in.

"I know you did something with my Cheetos."

"Huh?" The troll cackled and ran out of the room ahead of Leira. "He's going to figure out what you've been doing eventually," she said as the troll kept running up the stairs to his room on the second floor.

Leira took the stairs two at a time behind him, dodging the broken one near the top of the first set of stairs. Yumfuck turned to the left and went in his room shutting the door.

Leira continued up the stairs, turning into what passed for the master bedroom, pulling off her damp t-shirt and stripping down to her underwear.

"You can just stay like that." Correk came in and gently shut the door with his boot, wrapping his arms around Leira.

"We won't get much done if I do."

"We'll get something done."

She leaned into him and laughed. "Finally, something worth all the sweating," she said, pulling off his shirt.

———

Leira pulled a clean t-shirt and a pair of old jeans from the dresser and pulled the t-shirt over her head. "Time to tackle the kitchen."

"You're not big on spooning afterwards."

"Not till there's AC. Unless you've changed your mind about badabingbadaboom." Leira let the ends of her finger glow.

"We made that decision together. No magic."

"Just checking. In that case, we'll spoon in November." She stepped into her jeans zipping them up and stopped to look at the crowded row of framed pictures on the top of the tall dresser. She picked up the first one of Hagan and his wife, Rose standing in front of a blossoming rose bush in the forest sanctuary. *I'm glad I found them refuge.*

Rose looked healthier and happier than ever, and even Hagan looked thinner without a nearby donut shop. "I need to go see Hagan. It's been too long."

"Bring donuts. He'll act like he's fine with it, but he'll be thinking about them for the first fifteen minutes you're there. You can take Yumfuck too. That will really give him room to run." Correk nudged her over and pulled out a shirt, slipping it over his head. He put on a pair of jeans and got down to search for his boots under the bed.

Leira set the picture down and looked at the one next to it, a feeling of sadness gathering in her stomach. *Ossonia.* The Light Elf was standing at the edge of Oriceran's Dark Forest, smiling. It was from better days, long before she was sucked into the world in between. Leira swallowed hard and set the picture down as Correk put his chin on her shoulder. She leaned her head against his, still staring at Ossonia's smile.

"I haven't given up," said Leira.

"I know, and neither have I, but there are elements out of our control. Like your grandmother has reminded us more than once, Ossonia isn't going anywhere. We will get her out, but it has to be the right time and place."

"Perrom's never going to forgive me."

"Sure he will." Correk stood up straight. "Like everything else, it takes time. Paris changed everything, and not just for them. Our old lives ended after that battle, whether we knew it or not. Too much death and no real winners."

She turned around and hugged him. "I'm heading downstairs. I need a kitchen that works." She opened the bedroom door and went running down the stairs. Correk leaned over the railing. "No one in this house knows how to cook."

"We can learn," she called back, banging on Yumfuck's door as she passed by.

By the time they were all gathered in the kitchen at the back of the house she had pulled out a box of garbage bags and filled a bucket with soapy water.

"All right men, this kitchen is going to need a complete overhaul, but first let's just make it a little less disgusting. I think that's a layer of bacon grease and smoke on the walls."

"That could work." Yumfuck took a tentative lick and shrugged his tiny shoulders.

Leira shook her head and scooped him up, passing him off to Correk. "Hold on, Yoda. I think I can handle this one. Not sure even your stomach could take it."

"Come here, buddy. Let her show off a little," Correk leaned against the door frame and Yumfuck leaned a paw against the side of Correk's head.

Leira peered out the kitchen window at the small backyard patio and the rear of the house behind them. The pavers on the patio were broken, and she knew they would have to do it by hand since the neighbors would be able to see everything. *We'll get there.*

Yumfuck pressed *Stop* on his new stereo, ending the steady flow of nature sounds coming from the speakers. He took a deep breath and kept his eyes closed as his furry chest slowly rose and fell. He sat perfectly still for a moment, his hands in Vitarka Mudra just like the statue next to him that was a foot taller. He opened his eyes and looked at the Buddha just as his stomach loudly growled.

"To cure the hunger within one must bite the Cheetos." Yumfuck trilled, hopping off the twelve inch meditation mat and running to his closet. He crawled through Ninja turtle gear, hopping over a rolled up poster of the last season of Big Brother and landed behind a moving box. In the small gap between the box and the wall was a stash of Cheetos snack-sized bags, piled on top of each other. "Only nine left. I'll have to resupply soon."

He grabbed a bag, backing out of the closet and licked his lips, plopping down on the floor to open the bag. "Anticipation is the best part." He crawled inside and crunched down, flurries of orange dust flying out of the bag. It wasn't long before the entire bag was eaten. "Not a bad life. Ooooh still hungry." He rubbed his belly, streaks of neon-orange cheese smearing his fur.

Yumfuck stood up and grew to three feet tall, shaking all over, creating a shower of orange dust. He climbed onto a chair at his desk that mimicked the twisted wood of the giant trees in the Dark Forest of Oriceran. A gift to the troll from Jackson.

The windows were outfitted with heavy dark curtains to prevent prying eyes, and the bed included a small pull-out with his own supply of women's panties perfect for naps. In the corner was his favorite fern, the dirt piled to one side where he had created a divot for himself in the moist soil.

He pulled a pen, a piece of paper and an envelope out of the desk, pushing down a pile of letters from Hagan so he could shut the drawer. The Gardener of the Dark Forest made a point of postmarking them with the green outline of a stamp and the date.

Dear Hagan, he wrote. *I haven't found a new hidey hole yet, but I will before you visit. Something dark with good onion rings and a pool table. Thank you for the lock pick set, rope and the spade. They were just what I wanted and will come in handy when I'm out on patrol. No, I didn't tell L&C. We made a deal and I'm not a rat. I'm a troll. Please tell Rose thank you for the new capes and masks in two sizes. I'm really diggin having a short stack size and something to fit this three feet of awesome and I like knowing I can stay in disguise. I miss you big dude and I'll see you soon.*

Your best friend,

Yumfuck Tiberius Troll

He folded the letter and put it in the envelope, licking the flap and mashing it down with his paw to make sure it stuck. He left it propped in the corner of the picture with him and Mara Berens smiling at the camera. The troll was blowing a raspberry.

"Gonna save the world today." He grabbed his new sunglasses off the desk and hopped off the chair. "But first, lunch."

CHAPTER THREE

W olfstan stood a distance from the dark forest, on the far side of the royal gardens patiently waiting. He was hidden by the labyrinth, east of the floating castle and just off the far corner of the gardens. At his feet lay a dead Light Elf from the Dark Market who was never good at paying his debts.

"This will make us even, Gringle," said Wolfstan, nudging the Elf's cold hip with his boot.

Queen Saria came into the gardens, alone as usual, at the same time she always passed through. The corners of Wolfstan's mouth curled up at the edges. "Have to love a woman who knows how to be on time. Don't you agree?" He nudged the lifeless body again.

Wolfstan crouched next to the body and pulled out a leather drawstring pouch, loosening the strings. He pulled out soil mixed with ash and blew it over the dead elf's face whispering, "Quid est, iterum. Sine anima sunt vocem novum." It was an old, forgotten spell, unknown even to Rhazdon and the darkest of magic.

The dead body stirred, not taking in a breath. Its eyes opened but were pale and without an iris. "Stand up," Wolfstan whispered gently. His voice echoed out of the Elf's mouth as the body stood, stretching to its full stature. He leaned close and whispered in Gringle's ear. "Testing, one, two, three." He grinned, listening to his voice echo out of Gringle's gaping mouth. "This should be fun." He swallowed a laugh, draping a dark red shroud over Gringle's head, hiding most of his graying face. "Go find the queen."

Wolfstan opened his hand as a small, green ball of light grew in his palm. He threw it up in the air and watched it bob nearby in the adjoining garden. "Off with you."

The late Gringle walked flat footed out of the meditation garden through an iron gate, swaying slightly from left to right. Wolfstan looked up at the green ball, waiting for the color to grow brighter. *Bingo.*

He pulled in just enough magic, his fingers glowing and rubbed his neck, disguising his voice into a throaty rumble. "Hello my queen."

He heard her gasp over the thick brick wall and smiled again. "No need to be alarmed. I'm a proxy."

"I know what you are. I know the stories. But how?" She sounded angry more than afraid.

I think I like her.

"Doesn't matter. Not really the point. This isn't a show of my powers. It's a trade."

"Show yourself if you want to trade with me. Don't send your helpless ghoul. I don't deal with intermediaries, even dead ones."

"I know where you can find Harkin." Wolfstan looked at the dark green light. The queen wasn't moving. *Good.*

"But I want something for my information."

"Fool. I'll find him myself." The light dimmed as she started to walk away.

"No, you won't. Powerful forces are hiding him out of your reach." Wolfstan spit out the words, watching the light grow dimmer. "You never got to put your hands around the neck of your son's killer. Must be frustrating. Care for a second chance?" The light brightened again.

"Fraekin was an old friend, wasn't he?"

"Get on with it," snapped the queen.

Wolfstan licked his lips. "I want something in return. I want a place in the royal court. I want a seat at the table."

The queen let out a bitter laugh. "That will be a little hard without knowing who you are."

"You will when the time is right. But first, I want your word. I know you have never broken it."

There was a long pause and Wolfstan pressed a finger to his lips, patiently waiting. The hardest part.

"Tell me what you know. If the information is good, I'll give you access. That's it. Take it or leave it."

"Deal." Wolfstan squeezed his hands together in delight. "He's being hidden by the mythical Gardener of the Dark Forest on a sanctuary outside of Austin, Texas on the other planet."

"I have no say there," she spit out angrily. "I have no jurisdiction in that damnable forest. It's another realm."

"A minor detail that I may be able to give some assistance. Were you looking to bring him back for trial?" There was no answer. "I didn't think so. Peyton a friend too, wasn't he? The bodies pile up around Harkin. I'll be in touch."

Wolfstan let the green light extinguish and heard a thump as Gringle hit the ground, finally set loose to rest in peace.

Hagan patted his belly, frowning. "I haven't been to a grocery store in weeks. No impulse buying. No side trips to Voodoo Donuts. It's not American. I'm wasting away to nothing."

Harkin looked up from his makeshift workbench, his eyes glowing. "We may have different definitions of nothing."

Hagan pushed his chair away from the virtual screen tracking magical activity and rolled closer to Harkin. "Do they have donuts on Oriceran? Tell me one really good thing to eat that didn't fall off a tree or a bush."

Harkin watched the liquid grow around the circuit board taking shape as a smile grew across his face. "Progress sometimes comes in micro steps."

"What?" Hagan got up and came to take a closer look. "Looks like you're growing electronic jellyfish."

"You are not that far off except it's electronic musculature and a lot more complex."

"Sounds like I was a mile off." Hagan hitched up his pants and looked around the room, trying to figure out what to say. "Look, I know you've had a rough go of it for, what a hundred years or so."

Harkin looked up with an arched brow but went back to injecting magic into the liquid.

"But I heard about how you took responsibility for all

of it. That's all you can ask of somebody." He took out a white handkerchief and wiped his forehead. "I mean, Correk will come around. Berens was a tough case. Not that I'm her dad, but I was kind of her mentor."

Harkin stood up straight. "Pep talks are not your strong suit."

"Boy, you said it. Leira hated them. I think I only tried it twice." He put out his hand to shake. "But I meant every word."

"What do you want me to do? Do I hand you something?"

Hagan's eyebrows went up and he waggled his fingers in the air. "Really? In magicky land there's no such thing as a handshake? Interesting."

Harkin looked up at Hagan and narrowed his eyes. "You are very sincere even if you are at times very awkward." He turned back to his work. "I am not supposed to tell you, but Lois left a stash of candy for you in case of emergency. I couldn't figure out what would make up a candy emergency but maybe this is it."

"Well?" Hagan turned in a circle in the room. "Am I hot or cold?"

"You look hot. You're sweating profusely." He pointed with a wrench. "The candy is in that cabinet with the glasses. It's hidden behind them."

Hagan stabbed a finger in the air. "You and me, we just might be friends. I don't suppose you drink beer or play pool?"

An alarm went off, splitting the air and startling Hagan. "Mother of... every goddamn time!" His head whipped around to look up at the screen. Symbols were flying across it etched in red. "Oh, this is not good. The fucking dark families are at it again." He rubbed the top of his head trying to keep up with the flashing symbols, reading them as fast as he could. "I could swear that said assassin... headed to..."

Harkin dropped the wrench with a loud rattle, standing up straight and tying his longbow to his back in one swift movement. "It says an assassin from the dark families has a bounty on Correk. They're headed to the townhouse in DC."

"Where the hell... Never mind. I'd be doing the same. I get it. It's your kid no matter how many centuries go by. Do me a favor and be careful."

Harkin already had a portal open to the alley behind the Georgian building and was stepping through. "Warn Leira and Correk," he said, before he was all the way through, the portal already closing behind him, spitting out sparks.

"Like those two wouldn't already know. Damn, now I'm not even hungry," he said, dialing his phone. "Little buddy? Listen, trouble is headed your way. Warn the folks."

CHAPTER FOUR

Q ueen Saria stood at the window looking out over the gardens. Everything looked so peaceful. "It's a lie," she muttered. The vines along her crown were a deep green with buds at the edges that were refusing to bloom.

"Your Highness." A nervous Light Elf in the royal blue colors stayed near the door just in case he needed to make a hasty retreat.

"What is it?" She gazed out at the mountains, her irritation growing. She snapped her fingers, her back to him. "Spit it out."

"We received a card from a carrier pigeon. It has an address on Earth printed on it and it says to tell you. That was it. Oh!" His face brightened at remembering a small detail. "It also had printed at the very bottom, one hour. That was it. No explanation," he said with a shrug.

The queen lifted her chin, breathing harder. "Send two of our guards to that address. Do it now. Don't let me find out there was a delay. Tell them to bring me Harkin, dead or alive. I'm tired of playing games." She pressed her hand against the cold window but turned when she realized she could still hear the Elf muttering something.

"Go!" she shouted.

His body shook and he ran out of the room, shouting, "Altrea Extendia!"

"So much darkness these days. It all started with Rhazdon," said the queen, staring out at the mountains again. "But who will it end with... and when?"

Yumfuck hung up the phone and went searching through the townhouse, sliding down the rail on his feet with his toes hanging over the edge. He got to the foyer and jumped down to the floor, stopping to listen. No sounds.

The troll made his way to the kitchen where there was a note that Leira and Correk were walking to the corner store to stand by the freezer section and wouldn't be gone long.

"Home alone. I've got this. We defend the home." He started down the hall but was shoved over from behind by a pulse of energy moving through the lower floor. Someone was trying to penetrate the wards. "No time for a mask and cape this time."

He pressed up close to the baseboard, running back into the kitchen and toward the source of the pulse. He got up on the counter stepping on a bowl of avocados and peered out the kitchen window. "You are not what I was expecting."

In the alley stood a bespectacled young wizard with

tousled hair and a pleasant face quietly trying different spells.

"This is the assassin? They must have used a Groupon." Yumfuck watched as the wizard patiently tried one spell after another, bombarding the townhouse. At best he was rattling the dishes in the cupboards, but the wards were holding steady.

A portal opened behind him and Yumfuck slapped his paws against his face, watching Harkin bound through the opening, his longbow at the ready. "You are not supposed to be here." Yumfuck pressed his face up against the glass.

The teenager turned toward Harkin, his wand raised. But instead of going on the attack, he threw up a shield in defense and retreated down the alley.

"That was quick. That was too quick. No... no, no, no. Don't lower your bow, Harkin." Yumfuck pounded on the window with his paw, getting Harkin's attention. He shook his furry little head, but Harkin looked confused and walked closer to the townhouse, only to be rebuffed by the wards.

A blinding flash of light lit up the alley behind Harkin as he threw his arm over his eyes. Yumfuck squeezed his eyes shut and stepped back from the window, pressing himself against the backsplash. He pushed off and leaped for the edge of the counter, landing on his feet on the ground.

Crash!

There was the sound of glass breaking outside, followed by shouting as Yumfuck grew to three feet tall. Big enough to open the back door. He ran out the door, shrinking back down and slipped through the wards.

Two guards wearing the royal symbol for Oriceran on their tunics were moving in on Harkin, backing him up against the wards and leaving him no room to maneuver.

"I don't want to harm you," he was shouting, peppering them with fireballs meant to push them back, more than wound them.

Yumfuck ran into the space between the guards and Harkin and grew to his full stature of eight feet tall, his claws already bared, roaring in their faces. It was just enough to make them hesitate and gave the troll enough time to place his hand squarely on Harkin's chest and push him through the wards. They were designed to let any of the residents take someone through as long as there was contact.

Harkin fell backward but quickly got back up, ready to pass back through the wards and get back in the fight but Yumfuck blocked his way.

"Out of our way troll. We aren't after you."

"You come for someone in my family, you come for me and I always answer a threat. Looks like today I'm here for you." The troll stomped the ground, shaking it and letting out a roar, moving in on the two guards. The larger of the two guards curled his lip and formed a fire-ball in his hands, reaching back to throw it. An arrow sailed by his ear from behind, nicking the skin and star-tling him. The magical fire slipped out of his hand and hit the ground, burning a hole in the asphalt and fizzling out.

"Next time I aim just an inch to the left."

The royal guards spun around, more fire growing in the palms of their hand. At the end of the alley Correk had another arrow cocked and ready to go. Leira stood by his side, her eyes glowing.

"We have orders from the queen, Correk. Don't interfere."

"My father has my protection. Tell Queen Saria whatever she's been told, it was a carefully crafted lie. On my honor, I give you my word."

"We can't leave without him. Dead or alive."

Correk pulled the string tighter. "Then you don't leave. Your choice."

Leira formed a ball of fire in her hands and pulled at it till it was shaped like a glowing boomerang. She whispered an intention into it and tossed it, whipping it through the air. It circled the guards, creating rings of fire that extended down to the ground. "Hold very still. That fire will burn till I put it out. If it touches you, it will eat through your bones."

The guards glanced at each other, the larger one clenching his teeth. "Your word as a member of the court?"

"My word and my honor. I will bring her majesty the proof myself."

Leira blew out a puff of air and the flames bent slightly inward toward the guards. They looked behind them and saw the oversized troll, growling at their backs.

"Your only exit is going to be a portal, right where you stand," said Leira, tilting her head to the side. "But double back and I won't play so nice the next time."

The guards reluctantly opened a portal, careful not to get near the blue flames and stepped through, into the royal gardens. The smaller guard looked back at the last moment. "Fuck you, Jasper Elf," he said as it snapped shut.

"Not very royal," said Leira, letting the flames thin out till they were gone. "That was it? Fuck you, Jasper Elf? What, was he twelve? Not even a threat. That was actually kind of disappointing."

"Where did you learn to make an eternal flame?" Correk secured his bow and was running after Leira down the alley toward the townhouse and Harkin.

"I didn't. I was lying, but it was a good one. I even sucked you in with it. Old detective trick. Hagan would have loved it."

Yumfuck leaned down and patted Harkin on his head, but Harkin batted away the oversized paw. "I'm not a child. Why does your paw smell like cheese?"

Correk slowly looked up with an arched eyebrow. "You and I are going to chat later."

Yumfuck smiled, circling him and leaning over to bat at Correk's shoulder. "That can be arranged. Did anyone ever tell you, you're beautiful when you're angry?"

"I take it we've moved on to John Wayne movies." Leira shrugged when Correk scowled in her direction. "You realize they never run out of Cheetos. Ever. Anywhere."

"That's not the point."

"What is the point?" Harkin leaned back against the neighbor's brick wall. He let out a sigh, his brow furrowed. "I was worried about you, you know."

"This is kind of our life in a nutshell," said Leira. "Battles with dark forces mixed with plenty of junk food. I can't explain it, but it seems to work." She gave him a crooked smile. "Our own brand of magic."

"A well balanced diet." Harkin crossed his arms over his chest with a smirk.

"Correk, I think your dad just made a joke. This calls for a breakfast taco. On me."

"This isn't over Yumfuck." Correk walked past him opening the kitchen door, keeping his eye on the troll. "I want justice."

"Out here due process is a bullet."

"I don't know. I still wonder if we should put a parental guard on the TV. Okay, family meeting is over. Let's get out of this alley before a neighbor sees us and we have to explain we're redoing Shakespeare with an alien twist." Leira gave Harkin a nudge, nodding. "You too."

"We have to do something about Wolfstan."

"I know and we will after we get you back to the sanctuary. Right now, this is the part where we take a break and eat a taco."

"I want two!" Yumfuck let out a cackle and quickly shrunk down to five inches, scurrying between Correk's feet and disappearing inside.

CHAPTER FIVE

"Duty calls." Correk held up his phone. "Gotta take this."

"Why does Turner text you? Shouldn't he be able to mind meld with you?" Leira dried a bowl and put it in the cupboard.

"That's not a thing. I gotta go." He kissed Leira on the top of her head and opened a portal.

"That counts as magic inside the house."

"True. Love you and I'll see you later."

"You're like a magic fireman. Bell rings, you go." The portal closed just as she got out the last words. Leira turned back to the cabinets, ready to take on some serious renovating. *Time to make this feel like home.*

A loud bang overhead made her look up and pause. It was followed by the sound of tiny running feet. "Sorry," yelled Yumfuck, leaning over the railing on the second floor.

"How sorry? I broke something we can replace at Target

sorry? Or I ripped out part of a wall and this is gonna suck sorry?"

"Somewhere between those two, pardner."

"John Wayne doesn't work on me. Clean it up please, whatever it is."

More running feet and something heavy sliding across the floor, followed by another loud bang, and more running feet. "Sorry again."

"Fuck me." Leira weighed her options. *If I go upstairs, I have to deal with it.* "Is anyone bleeding or otherwise injured?"

"No."

Leira pursed her lips, thinking about the possibilities. "Has any dark magic escaped or morphed or something else horrible I haven't thought to ask?"

There was a long pause.

"Uh... no."

"Don't fuck with me troll. I know where you hid the Cheetos evidence. I'm willing to rat you out to Correk to get revenge for whatever you're doing to the house."

"How about, no by the time you come upstairs?"

Another long pause.

"I can live with that. Are you... Never mind, I don't want to know." Leira went back to fixing the door on the cabinet so it didn't hang at an angle. "It's like I have a kid that will never age," she muttered, "and can rip someone's head off with one swipe." She stopped working and thought about that for a moment, walking out to the hallway and leaning back to look up the stairs. "Are you sure you're okay up there?"

"I'm sure I'm okay. But give me a little time before you come up here."

"You have an hour."

"That should do it."

Leira stayed where she was for a moment, the screwdriver in her hand. "Nope, I'll give him an hour. What could go wrong in an hour?" She shook her head. "I'm going to forget I said that."

Wolfstan Humphrey sat in the small dining room inside the White House run by the Navy. At the table covered in a starched white tablecloth were Senator Thatcher and Senator McCauley, another long-standing member of the Senate. Both men sat on the Armed Service Committee.

Senator Thatcher waved to the waiter in a white jacket, lifting his white coffee cup and saucer. He put them back down and narrowed his gaze, watching Wolfstan. Senator McCauley sat back in the wooden chair, crossing his hands in his lap over his white cloth napkin. "We appreciate the generous support you've given to both Senator Thatcher and myself, but I don't see how we can assist you. You're not in our jurisdictions and we don't have any say over what the FDA approves."

Wolfstan slowly drummed his fingers on the tablecloth. "Fleeker is a large corporation that got its start in biotechnology, but we are expanding. We're taking our roots and looking for more applications in the real world. It's the only way to stay relevant."

Senator Thatcher gave a sidelong glance to Senator

McCauley, the lights in the dining room shining off his thinning silver hair.

"I take it since you specifically asked for the two of us and are doing a pretty damn fine job of courting us, your new avenue has weapons applications," said Senator McCauley, warily.

"Research and development, specifically." Wolfstan paused dramatically, leaning back and smiling. He leaned forward again, slapping the table. "I understand you two have some knowledge of magic returning to Earth from Oriceran."

Senator Thatcher still said nothing, his expression blank. There was a reason he had lasted in political life as long as he had. There was never a reason to rush an opinion on anything.

"Continue," said Senator McCauley, pursing his lips.

"Magic is wonderful, I highly recommend it," said Wolfstan, creating a small ball of light in his hands and quickly extinguishing it with the other. "But even that has its limits. There are rules. Of course, dark magic has fewer rules and can be more fun, but the consequences can have a real sting."

Neither man moved at all, carefully watching Wolfstan. The waiter came and refilled the coffee without saying a word, leaving the men to their negotiations.

"Tough room, I get it. To be good at politics, you have to understand all the angles at once. How it will affect your constituents in every given scenario. Magic is new to you and it's something you can't do. It's impossible to predict how this will all turn out. Still..." He leaned forward conspiratorially. "It has rules, which means they can be learned, harnessed."

"What does this have to do with us?"

"The limitations. It turns out that while the gates were closed all this time, humans were busy creating all kinds of new inventions with all kinds of vast applications. Technology has made great leaps and bounds. What if we could combine the two? Mix magic and technology to create new weaponry. Even better, what if we took those two categories and mixed them with organic matter?"

Senator Thatcher shifted in his chair, leaning forward ever so slightly. Wolfstan felt a thrill rising in his chest. His second seat of power was so close.

"We could prolong life, repair damage, create more powerful soldiers. There are so many applications."

"Wait a minute." Senator McCauley looked around to see who was close enough to hear them and leaned in, talking in a low voice. "Are we talking about modifying human beings with technology?"

"And magic. Whole new avenue that can give people strength and endurance they've never known before. Animal testing has already begun, and we'd like to partner... with someone." Here was the crucial part of his pitch.

Senator Thatcher rubbed his hands together and cleared this throat. "What is it you would want in exchange? What's the price tag for this whole new world order? That is what we're talking about, am I right?"

Senator McCauley's eyes widened, and he grew pale, but said nothing.

"It's expensive, of course. New ideas of this magnitude generally are, but I will be reasonable. Of course, I'd like to help advise on how best to use the new invention." He said the last word slowly. "My unique background could prove very useful. To someone."

"I get the veiled threat, Mr. Humphrey," said Senator Thatcher, his eyes hooded and his expression still veiled.

"Not a threat at all. That's why I've come to you first. I'd prefer to deal with the US, but if you're going to take a pass..."

"We're interested. Of course we're interested, but we'll need a lot more information to move forward even an inch." Senator Thatcher felt the bile rise in his throat. *First Charlie Monaghan goes off the rails and disappears and now someone is building soldiers out of spare parts. What next?*

"Why don't we start with a tour of Fleeker, just outside of Austin, Texas. I think you will see the potential to dominate the world stage and craft the foreign policy you'd like to see well ahead of the gates fully opening and an entire new world to negotiate with."

"My office can arrange it with you. But let's be clear, this is not an approval of anything. Just an inquiry."

"Understood and more than enough," said Wolfstan Humphrey with a grin that spread across his face. He could barely contain his elation.

CHAPTER SIX

S parks shimmered and fizzed behind Correk as he stepped through the portal onto a freshly mowed lawn. The backyard of the old Victorian-style home was in a neighborhood outside of Wichita and shielded on all sides by eight-foot-tall fences.

All around the yard were small statues, some of them fairies, others the typical human's idea of a lawn gnome.

A small section of the yard was cordoned off with chicken wire. "This must be the place." He raised an eyebrow, watching the swaying flowers move in time with his voice.

"A witch in distress with illegal Oriceran plants in the backyard. Poor decision making skills may have gotten you here, ma'am."

He took two steps forward but was stopped dead in his tracks in surprise.

A rush of dark magic hit him, pushing out the breath in his lungs. He pulled in air, gritting his teeth and standing his ground, scanning the property. A trail of dark magic was seeping from a set of double doors covering a storm cellar. Small billows of smoke were seeping from the cracks with an acrid stench that burned.

Correk tapped the metal handles to make sure they weren't hot and opened one of the doors, dropping it open to the side. The old rusted hinges squeaked as he pulled open the other, covering his mouth as the smoke billowed out.

There was a faint groan coming from deep inside the shelter. Correk felt the pull of the magical's cry for help, the pulse of energy pushing out. The stream of energy from every magical that connected them to the Fixer constantly reaching out, sending alerts. Correk briefly shut his eyes and turned his head slightly to the east, smelling the air. So many requests.

"The witch is still top of the list, for ten more minutes at least."

Correk swept his hand in front of his face, pushing away the smoke. He made his way down the steps, kicking a metal bucket that went clanging down the cement steps. Thorny vines were writhing across the floor, some of them turning toward the sound, crawling over Correk's boots. "Pariter ut vestri reditus."

The vines withered into ashes around his boots. Three enamel pots were bubbling on hot plates on a wooden table covered in a red tablecloth. Next to them was a plastic water bottle holding the same bubbling liquid.

A moan arose from the other side of the table and Correk rushed around to find a middle-aged witch with her hands crumpled against her chest.

"You really got yourself into this one." A broken vial was

emitting more dark smoke that was rolling across the tabletop. "Playing with dark magic? You could be arrested by the Silver Griffins." He glanced back over his shoulder. "Or end up dead... or worse."

"I needed it," she gasped. "The darkness is coming. I needed protection."

Her eyes rolled back in her head and she began to shake. Small blisters spread up her neck, oozing a dark liquid onto her skin. Correk got on one knee and closed his eyes, mentally sorting through the different spells he had learned. "No, that one won't work." He shook his head. "This one will take that odd spell Turner insisted I learn."

Correk held his hands over the witch's body. "Reversaro Intentus." Light from his palms raced over the witch's body, reading cells and transmuting just enough of them.

The shaking gradually slowed and the witch gasped, taking in a deep breath as her eyes opened wide. Correk rubbed his hands together and examined the burns on her legs. A dark cherry color was slowly making its way up the skin on her legs.

The spell isn't going to last much longer. "Can you talk?"

She nodded, blinking her pale blue eyes.

"What spell were you trying to do?"

She opened her mouth, but only a squeak came out. She shut it again and closed her eyes, tears squeezing out the sides.

"Come on, I need you to muster the strength to tell me." Correk pressed his fingers against her shoulder, trying to calm her energy.

The witch shook her head, opening her eyes and calming her breathing despite the dark red ooze spreading further up her body. She reached into her pocket and pulled out a piece of paper, holding it out for Correk.

"Respillum nevor..." He whispered only a few more words, stopping before he got to the end. "This magic is before Rhazdon. How did you get it?"

She muttered something too quietly for Correk to hear. He leaned down closer and she whispered, "The Earth has its own dark market."

"How is that possible and I don't know about it?"

"It's all virtual. On the internet. Kind of clever," she choked out, pulling her crooked fingers closer to her chest. The bones were beginning to curl and splinter and the toes on her feet were turning under.

That's the second time now. "Clever till someone turns themselves into a pretzel." He bit his lower lip and flexed his fingers, wondering if he should try the counter spell. The witch cried out in pain from the bones cracking.

I have no choice. Two moons. He positioned his hands over her body again. "Alzalam yatalashaa. Yamla aldaw' alfaragh."

The light from his palms grew brighter, moving over the witch's body. She stiffened with a gurgle, the darkness in her veins breaking into bits, pinging around just under her skin. A thin stream of black liquid formed a puddle beneath her.

The witch's hands were unfurling, and her toes were stretching out, lessening her agony. She breathed deeply and looked up at Correk, shadows under her eyes. "What was that spell?" She tried to lift her head, falling back against the floor.

"Darkness fades. Light fills the void." It was one of the oldest known spells.

"That is so much better," she croaked. "Thank you."

"You may not survive your next dark spell. Try simple wards. They work well enough." Correk crouched down to help her sit up and rest her back against the table leg.

"Not well enough for what's coming."

"What's coming?"

"Darkness. The rumors are everywhere among the magicals. Someone is taking our kind and experimenting on them, but it's not the humans."

Correk rocked back on his heels. "It's begun," he muttered. A pull of magic in the stream caught his attention, and he turned his head, centering on the one magical among many reaching out to him.

It was Harkin.

"I have to go." Correk helped the witch to her feet and sat her in a chair. "No more dancing on the dark side." He waved his arm over the pans and the water bottle. "Pariter ut vestri reditus." The contents turned to ashes, vaporizing into mist. "If you have any more spells, bury them in dirt and soon. There's still a chance a Silver Griffin will show up here with a lot of questions."

The witch saluted Correk. "Don't have to tell me twice. This was bad enough. Go on, I know you have other house calls."

Correk started to open a portal but stopped at the last minute. "Can you show me how to get on the dark web? Quickly?"

"Yeah, it'll take about two minutes. Hang on, my phone's stuck in my back pocket. It's an app but you have to know the spell to make the app work." She scrolled through her phone till she got to a thumbnail sized picture of two moons. Both of them were dark new moons with a thin outline of light.

Correk looked over her shoulder, a scowl on his face. "I'll be needing that spell too."

CHAPTER SEVEN

L eira teetered on one foot on the step ladder, unscrewing the broken fire alarm from the ceiling.

"Oof. What the fuck?" The soles of her feet grew icy cold, prickling with pins and needles. She jumped off the ladder, her eyes glowing, with two fingers in her mouth about to whistle for the troll but stopped short at the sight of the old Fixer in the doorway.

"Seriously, dude." She put her hand to her chest, the magic fading. "You have got to quit sneaking up on people like that."

Turner Underwood leaned on the silver bird topping his cane, giving a sly smile with a tan felt Homburg firmly on his head.

Leira leaned back and took a second look at the older Light Elf. "You look tired. How is that possible? You're supposed to be doing less."

"There's still plenty for me to do. I needed to check on my star student. Why haven't you been returning my calls?" Turner made his way to the red velvet chair.

"A long and weird to-do list," Leira replied, hopping off the ladder. "Dead fathers coming back. Dark wizards setting traps."

"So I see." He pointed the end of his cane at the bruises visible above Leira's t-shirt. "That looks fresh. What happened?"

"Sirius happened." Leira shrugged it off. "He took the worst of it."

Turner raised a bushy eyebrow and leaned his cane against the side of the chair, pressing his fingertips together near his lips and staring at Leira.

She stared back, playing out Hagan's rule. *Whoever speaks first loses.*

"You haven't been by the house for an official tour," said Turner.

"That's a dodge. I've come by a couple times. Why are you really here?" Leira stood up and walked past him, shoving a box out of the way with her foot, heading toward the kitchen.

"Are we relocating?" Turner sighed and grunted as he lifted himself out of the chair, walking after her into the kitchen, tapping his cane.

Leira watched how he was carrying himself. "You've been up to something. You're moving like you've been in a battle." She pulled a bottle of Dr. Pepper from the fridge and held it up to Turner, raising her eyebrows.

"No, thank you." He cleared his throat. "Not really my thing, though I do like a good cream soda."

"Dr. Pepper is made in Texas." Leira twisted off the top and took a sip, her eyes fixed on him. He smiled and looked at the floor, knowing she was waiting for something.

"Alright, I'll go first again." He rubbed his chin and settled back, his eyelids growing heavy. "I am tired."

Leira leaned against the old Formica counter, sipping the Dr. Pepper.

He glanced up at Leira. "I've been trying to help Peyton. Progress is very slow. It gives me pause when I think of what Wolfstan Humphrey is up to."

"He must have spent his entire time in Trevilsom Prison creating a fun mirror of a manifesto. He wants to connect all the dots. Oriceran's largest kingdom, this world's largest government, the corporate world, the dark families."

"Make them all bow to him."

"Who do you think kicked him around when he was a kid? It's the biggest chip on a shoulder I've ever seen." Leira finished the Dr. Pepper and put the bottle in the green recycling bin.

"It's up there, and with technology as a new wrinkle it has made things much more dangerous. You need someone on the inside of the operation." Turner rubbed his face. "That presents its own problems. Both sides have already thrown down so everyone's guard is up."

"We may already have someone."

Turner looked up, surprised. "A bit of good news I didn't see coming. That does not happen to me often enough." He sat forward, rubbing his hands together. "Who is it?"

"Lily Sharpton, a young witch who works at Fleeker in R&D. She's been there a while and knows nothing."

"The perfect plant."

"And Lois' niece."

"Huh, this day is turning around. A legacy no less."

"But we would be asking a young witch who has no tactical training to spy on the most dangerous magical I've ever met."

"My dear, if we don't do all we can, we will all be pulled into this fight anyway, but on the defense with a lot more horror. There is no question of whether or not we are all in it, it's about when and under what circumstances. Do you have an alternative?"

"No... no, I don't. I'll ask Lois. At least plant the seed because I don't see her saying yes, at first."

Turner Underwood rose out of his chair. "Come see what my oversized mansion can offer you and Correk while you're in DC. This remodeling you're doing can wait. Take a break with an old Light Elf."

"Pulling the old Light Elf card. That's low. Fine, it would be kind of nice to see the shiny doodads. Lead the way." Leira followed behind Turner who headed for the back door. "How did you get past all our wards?"

"Child's play for a Fixer."

"Oooh, does that mean Correk knows how to do that?"

"I taught Correk all my tricks, but it will take him years to make them his own and add nuance. Let's create the portal in the alley. Leave less of a trail."

Leira gave a crooked smile, stepping outside. "You didn't break all of the wards, did you?"

Turner let out a loud laugh and relaxed for the first time since he had gotten there. "No, you clever child, I did not. I saw that it was yours. Well done."

Turner stepped away from the walls of the townhouse and opened his hands, pulling apart an opaque bubble and creating a portal. A cool breeze hit Leira from the marble entryway of Turner's large house.

Leira shut her eyes, opening her arms wide. "AC! The best."

Turner walked into his foyer and waited, tapping his cane on the hard floor. "It's even better from in here."

Leira stepped through, the portal closing behind her with a loud zip.

"Welcome to my audacious home." He leaned on his cane with a tired smile. "No point in my trying to act humble. This is one of my favorite houses and it's badass," he said, leaning in with a wink.

"If you're saying *that* I'm going to assume there's hidden surprises I haven't seen that will delight and attack."

"All kinds of hidden things. I've owned it for over a hundred years, and I've had time to embellish. Come on, let's start with something simple."

He led Leira down the wide center hallway past a formal living room. Turner waved to it saying, "I only use that room to welcome dignitaries. They need the dog and pony show." He kept moving, walking past several other rooms that stretched down the hallway and came to a door on the right in the back corner that had no handle. He turned with a smile. "Now, here is where it gets interesting."

"Something new.Okay, you've teased it enough. Come on, show me the goods. How do we get in here?"

Turner's eyes glowed and he tapped on the door, a glass

handle appearing. He turned the knob, opening the door with a grin and waited for Leira to go first.

Leira peered inside. "Aren't you a little worried about overselling? No? Okay, I'm going." She stepped through the door and was surrounded by a cold mist in complete darkness. "You do know how to build excitement. Turner?" Her voice echoed making her eyes widen with curiosity. She stepped forward a few steps, a crooked smile growing and waved her arms, sensing nothing close by as she kept walking.

Behind her Turner Underwood let out a deep, belly laugh. "You are the first to have that reaction! Most inch forward, reluctant to go toward what they can't see. You are always a delightful surprise." He snapped his fingers sharply and the light gradually came up from the floor, rising toward the ceiling.

Leira's mouth dropped open and she took in a deep breath, slowing down to take it all in.

Laid out in front of her was another large building, much bigger than the one she had entered from the street, and much less formal. "It's spectacular," she whispered. Doors lined the long hallway and different sounds and lights were coming out of each one. "Are those explosions?" Leira spun around, her brows knit together. "Was that sound a whale? Is that possible?"

Turner laughed again, the strain on his face easing. "Anything is possible. Always remember that."

"You made your own version of a secret garden." Leira ran ahead, disappearing into the first room on the left.

"Okay, don't wait for me," Turner chuckled. "Love that girl." He moved with a lighter step, still tapping his cane along the ground and followed Leira into the oversized gym. "It's ten thousand square feet with thirty foot ceilings," he shouted.

"This makes the gym you have in the main house look kind of sparse." Leira was already at the other end, climbing the rope wall and leaning out to swing to the next course. "The wainscoting is a nice touch. A classy gym."

"I told you, I had time to make embellishments. I like nice things."

"I like that you like nice things." She jumped off the edge of a tall wooden block and grabbed onto a ring, letting go over a foam pit and crawling out, a grin on her face. "This is amazing!"

"This is nothing. This place is more of a necessity to keep me fit. The real fun is further down the hall."

"Then why are we standing here?" She ran ahead again, down the hall choosing the next door, which opened into a smaller room. It was a sparse room with only a tall mirror and a closet to one side. Leira turned to leave but Turner stopped her at the door.

"Don't be so quick. Take another look," he said with an arched brow.

Leira turned around and looked at the simple room again. "There's not much here."

"It doesn't matter how much is ever in front of you. It matters what they contribute."

"Oh, this is the best fucking day ever. A riddle for a detective without a gruesome ending." Leira opened the closet door and saw three empty hangars. She looked back at Turner, who shrugged. "Keep going."

She went and stood in front of the mirror and was

about to turn away when a ripple ran through the center of the mirror from the top to the bottom and back up again. Tiny beams of light shot out, scanning Leira's body and head, circling every inch and retracting back into the mirror.

"That was a little invasive."

Turner snorted with laughter watching her.

"I don't get it." Leira looked closer and stood back again. The mirror had returned to its sedate reflective state.

"Check the closet again."

Leira tilted her head to one side and slowly opened the closet, letting out a whoop of delight. Inside on one of the hangars was a black leather jacket with silver zippers along each pocket and a pair of black leather boots. "Hot damn. That is exactly what I would want."

"The mirror is an old artifact given to me as a gift a hundred years ago from a tailor. It reads your body *and* your mood and creates an outfit to suit both. In over a hundred years it's never been wrong."

Leira slipped into the jacket and ran her hand along the soft leather. "That's why you always look so dapper."

"Come on, the boots will be waiting for you at the front door when we're done. There is a lot more to see."

Leira spun around in a circle before running out of the room, dashing past Turner.

"Wait for me before you go in the next room. I want to be there when you see it," he said.

Leira slowed down and stood at the edge of the darkened and quiet room, waiting for Turner. "I'm surprised you spend so much time in Austin." A look of surprise came over her. "Wait! Is there more to the Austin house?"

"A surprise for another day."

"How did I not know any of this?"

"Very few are ever invited into my inner sanctums. Too much risk in my line of business."

Turner stepped over the threshold of the room and took in a deep breath, dramatically raising his arms and looking up. Leira came in and stood next to him and looked up.

Fireworks appeared overhead, exploding far above what should have been the ceiling.

"How is this happening?" Leira's eyes shined, the exploding colors reflecting in her eyes. "Reminds me when I was little, and Mom and Grandma were there, and we would go and see fireworks together." Her voice was barely above a whisper, full of wonder.

"It's like a planetarium, but for fireworks. It never fails to get me to relax. It's why I put in the movie seating." In the center of the room were two rows of leather recliners separated by cup holders.

"Wow, you are even cooler than I realized."

"Yes, I am," he said, smiling. "I love fireworks. There's even a snack station behind a panel." Turner Underwood waved his arm and the sky changed, stars appearing clearly overhead. "But sometimes a planetarium is nice too."

"When I grow up, I want to be you."

"That's already taken by your partner. But maybe he'll share."

"I have to talk Correk into all of this." Leira clapped her hands together. "Does it do anything else?"

Turner snapped his fingers and a meteor shower shot across the artificial sky.

Leira tilted her head back even further, her mouth open staring upwards. "How do you fit all this in here?" She looked around, calculating the size of what she had seen so far. "There isn't enough space on this block and we still haven't seen everything. Are we in a weird kind of portal?"

This time it was Turner whose bushy eyebrows went up with surprise. "That is an interesting thought. I may have to look into that to see if it's possible to make an enormous permanent portal act like a room of its own. Hmmm... Of course, there's that pesky problem of a tear leading to the world in between."

"Yeah, pesky problem. Okay, then what carnival trick have you pulled off?"

Turner shook a finger. "That is a great question. There is very powerful magic that is not dark magic but is still not known by many. It takes a lot of experience to practice and keep it stable."

"It's like you bent physics."

Turner tapped his nose, wandering out of the room. "Now you've got it. I knew you would understand. All of magic must work with the laws of physics. Powerful magic can bend it more. These rooms all exist in a small space that can fit in the palm of your hand," said Turner, holding out his hand. "What the magic does is expand that space on a different plane."

"Okay, I kind of get it. How many places are there like this?"

"Hard to say. Like I said, this is one of the most closely guarded secrets. The Silver Griffins know but only at the top levels and as far as I know it's only used when there's a new leader. So far, we've kept it out of the hands of the dark families. Come on, just a couple more rooms to show you. That will be enough for today at least."

Leira let out a sigh. "There's far more, isn't there." She grasped her hands in front of her chest. "The world is an amazing place and just when I think I have a handle on it, there's more to see and know and do."

"This is why you possess the energy of light inside of you. Your curiosity doesn't end."

"How does that explain my dad?"

"Ha! Good point. Here we are at the next stop. This room is more functional and best hidden from any prying eyes. This is the last resort room, which fortunately I have never had to use, yet."

Inside, the room was ringed with wooden and glass cabinets and inside were different types of rifles, automatic weapons, ground to air missiles, and a large variety of handguns. The smile slipped from Leira's face and she walked down the line with her hands on her hips. "I recognize all of these. That's a pretty good arsenal." She stopped halfway. "But what kind of weaponry is this? Looks like a twisted Nerf gun."

Turner came and stood by a cabinet that had large weapons hanging on pegs. "Advanced technology with a little magic added in. I'll teach you all about them, later. But you are to never use them unless everything else in the two worlds out there has failed. I want your word."

"Armageddon weapons, I get it. Okay, sure, you have my word. Why create them?"

"Because dark magic has a way of popping back up and

some day it may gain the advantage. We must be ready to take it back."

"Oof. I had forgotten for a minute about Wolfstan Humphrey."

"Then let's get out of this room and restore the day. The last two on today's tour are the best rooms of all."

"That's really saying something." Leira shook out her arms, letting the chill that had come over her pass. *Save it for the world out there.*

"I rarely get to show anyone this part of the house. I have to tell you," said Turner, the smile returning, "it's so much better to see it all through your eyes. This next room was created with the help of the Gardener of the Dark Forest. That's right, we have been known to collaborate together. One great Fixer of sorts to another."

"What kind of room would the two of you build?" Leira stepped through a doorway and was in a short hallway, immediately surrounded by a clear bubble that moved with her as she walked. "Is this it? Does something happen overhead?"

"No, keep going and through the double doors. Over there."

She pushed at the doors and exited the bubble, entering into an endless room, her ears popping from a change in air pressure. Ten feet above her was a clear barrier and above that an ocean of water teeming with marine life. "The whale sound."

Just over her head a grey whale swam by, filling her view, barnacles clinging to its belly. Leira stretched out her arm, waggling her fingers. "That is the most amazing thing I've ever seen. You created a marine sanctuary in a house."

"Well, technically in another plane, but yes, it's a sanctuary. The wet version of the Dark Forest and without human or magical interference. Completely hidden away. It's a balanced ecosystem too. It doesn't really need much help from me."

A school of blue and orange fish swam one way and turned slightly, swimming in a new direction. Leira could barely take it all in.

"Those are mandarinfish. The only fish with a true blue pigment. There are over twenty thousand species in this ocean we've created."

"There's a question I've had since I learned about magic and how long I may live." Leira watched the fish swim out of view and an octopus inch along the bottom, its purple suckers peeling on and then off the smooth surface. "I wondered if I would get bored at some point. But there's so much to be learned and so much to see."

"It won't even fill up an old Fixer's lifetime," said Turner, smiling. "This one was a doozy creating the stability to hold up an ocean, but it's the next one where so far I have outdone myself and really begs for more people to come and visit."

"Just a few more minutes." Leira's head was tilted back watching the octopus gracefully swim through the water. Her eyes began to glow, and the symbols lit up along her arms. Turner reached out and grabbed her shoulder, evening out her magic. "That is forbidden in here. No excess magic, and in particular yours. I can't be sure how it would affect things and I don't care to find out. There aren't enough paper towels in the world."

The glow in her eyes dimmed and she felt the energy subside. "Fair enough."

"Let's keep moving. There is more to see."

They went back into the hallway, passing back through the bubble and into the bigger hallway, arriving at what looked like a swinging door. "Have I ever told you my fondness for the nineteen hundreds in America? Oh, how I loved that time. Before the first world war when combustion engines were new, and innovation was everywhere. There was so much optimism. It was a perfect era."

"Is this nostalgia related to what I'm about to see?"

"It is everything. Okay, go inside." Turner brushed away a tear, smiling, making Leira's forehead wrinkle.

"I've never seen this side of you," she said softly, walking through the door. She froze for a moment, trying to take in what she was seeing. "Holy crap!"

"Welcome to New York City, but in 1905."

"Is the entire city in here?" Leira shook her head. "This is over the top, even for you. I... I don't know what to say. Fuck."

"Eloquent as ever. This is a recreation of just part of the city. The lower East Side to be exact. My old stomping grounds and full of so many memories for me."

"That is a wonderful smell," said Leira, lifting her chin and sniffing the air.

"That's coming from Katz' deli. An exact replica. I eat there as often as I can," said Turner, strolling down the street next to Leira.

"I thought you said this room was empty." Different magicals, all dressed in turn of the century clothes wandered the street. Some of them looked at Leira and her new leather jacket.

"No, I said there should really be more magicals. Right now, this is a town for refugees. Your grandmother has sent many of them to me. No one can detect them here."

"Harkin could live here."

"Harkin would never stay here. He grows restless too easily and he tends to want to improve on things. Harkin must never know of this world's existence. I assume I have your word on that."

"I gave it to you already. I'll keep it." Leira stepped back to let a horse drawn Hansom cab with the driver standing in the back pass by her. "I want to be the Fixer."

"You have a different calling. We are stopping at the townhouse just on the corner. There's someone I want you to meet."

Turner walked up the stone steps to a three story townhouse and a large door painted black with a large brass knocker in the center.

"Looks a lot like my new place," said Leira. "I'm getting the bends trying to integrate what I'm seeing with what I knew. I feel like I'm back in the floating palace."

Turner went inside, this time not waiting for Leira.

She took one last look around, smiling at a group of children running down the street after a dog before running up the steps and through the door. "Turner? Where did you go?"

She found him in the drawing room sitting on a settee. In an old leather Morris chair sat a weathered Light Elf in full leather battle gear, trying to set up a Roku to a flat screen TV.

"This doesn't fit at all. You can get cable in this place?"

"Yes, with surprisingly good coverage. Life doesn't have to be without amenities. It's an old city but it's not stuck in the past."

"Blast!" The Light Elf pushed a button on the remote, trying to get the ESPN channel.

"I don't know. It kind of messes with the vibe going on outside."

"It's not Westworld. Leira, I'd like you to meet the old King of Oriceran. Ignore the outfit. I haven't been able to convince him to try fitting in with everyone else."

The king harrumphed and stood to greet her, easily towering over Leira. "We meet again," he growled.

A shudder passed down Leira's spine. "I saw you in the world in between. I saw those other creatures pull you back."

"They did not prevail. You are the partner of Correk? I knew his grandfather, my best friend."

"Wow, fuck me. This is a lot of information coming at me."

The old king arched an eyebrow and glanced at Turner who shrugged and sat back, crossing his leg.

"The king may be able to help with Wolfstan. He knows some of Rhazdon's old magic."

"It was the only way to fight her. I had to learn to be her. Still, it didn't work for me. But you... a new kind of warrior." He looked Leira up and down. "Such a small being to possess so much magic."

"It's in concentrated form. Why are you hiding out in old New York City?"

"Not hiding out," growled the king, scowling. "Biding my time."

"The new king doesn't know yet."

"And I'm catching up with time," he said, picking up the remote. "And learning about baseball. I'm a Nats fan."

Leira shook her head. "Again, that's a lot of information." She pressed her hand to her belly. "I may be done for the day."

"This is a good stopping place. We will all meet up again and put together a strategy for Wolfstan Humphrey and Fleeker. We have a few things on our side that he doesn't know about, and best to keep that way."

"Peyton is in here too, isn't he?"

Turner pursed his lips, letting out a weary sigh. "Good observation. Yes, he's in here and learning the best he can how to fit in. It's still a problem keeping his energy stable, but we're working on it."

The king pushed a button again and the channel appeared, coming on in the middle of a baseball game. "Cardinals, hmph." He sat back down in the Morris chair, ignoring Leira.

"I suppose if I had been stuck in another realm full of goo for seven hundred years I'd be easily distracted too."

"Lucius has the same habit. Like a dog spotting a squirrel." Turner stood up, pushing on his cane. "Time to go back to what most consider the real world." He chuckled, shaking his head. "It's really a relative concept."

"This is really blowing my concept of everything. It feels like I'm at the top of a roller coaster looking over the edge."

Turner looked up delighted. "There's an area with one

of those too. The Hurler from Kings Dominion. And a Ferris wheel built by George Ferris. I love my life."

The pair made their way to the exit out of New York City and walked down the long hallway past all the doors.

"I'm coming back here... often. I can do a staycation here for weeks."

"And you'll have your own key to this area too. A magical key. If you approach the door with the key a lock will appear for you. This is why I've been trying to get you to come for a tour."

"I can come and go as I please in here?" Leira narrowed her eyes. "Do I need to wear a costume in some of these rooms?"

"Yes and no," he said, tossing her a key. "I'll show you how to get around the charms."

"And Correk?"

"I will give you the privilege of showing him the place. He will need to know it all because someday he will be the caretaker."

"Like he wasn't hot already." Leira hugged Turner around his neck. "Thank you."

Turner smiled and walked her out of the door and back into the hallway of the mansion.

"Try to stay away from the rogue wizards. For me."

"I'll do my best. They're usually looking for me, you know. Okay, not always."

Leira looked down at the key and gave a crooked smile. *Something good in the middle of all this. Wait till I tell Correk.* She shoved the key in her pocket and walked to the doorway.

"You stay away from any..."

She stopped mid-sentence and looked around the room. The only traces of Turner were the small round spots from his cane on the dusty hardwood floors.

"I take it I'm making my own portal home? How does he *do* that?"

CHAPTER EIGHT

Correk found Harkin in the town square of Hillsdale outside the pub drinking an ale with a Kilomea at a cafe table. The Kilomea looked up at Correk and grunted, curling his lip into a sneer. "The Fixer makes house calls down here too?"

"Not as often, but yes. This is still Earth." The artificial light streamed down on them.

"Barely." The Kilomea looked around, shrugging. "No one is in any danger here. Go rescue a small witch or a couple of Gnomes."

"There's more than one way to be in danger."

"He means me," said Harkin, taking a long swig of his foamy beer and wiping his mouth on his sleeve. "It's preemptive danger. He's come to rescue me before it happens." Harkin raised his hand, signaling the waitress he wanted another drink.

"A concierge service. That's new. How do I get in on that?" grunted the Kilomea.

Correk arched an eyebrow and reached into a pocket, pulling out the family ring and holding it up for Harkin to see. "We need to discuss this."

Harkin lowered his arm slowly and shook his head. "Now you have my attention. Finley, I'm afraid we're done for the day. I'll look for you here again." Harkin reached into a pocket to get a few pintas.

"No, these are on me," said Finley. "Good to see you again, Harkin." The Kilomea rose out of his chair and brushed past Correk. "Fixer," he said with a nod.

"Making new friends?" Correk sat down across from his father.

"Strange story. I knew him from Oriceran years ago and ran into him down here. What are the odds?"

"Very high and why you have to stay out of sight."

Harkin slapped his hand on the table. "Maybe I will get that beer. I'm not staying like a bird in a cage. I've done that enough in this very long lifetime."

Correk felt a sharp ache in his chest and sat back in his chair. "An entire sanctuary is not a cage."

"It's a controlled environment not of my making. Wolfstan's already won."

"Not by a long shot. If you want to be out here, we have to prove you're innocent. We have to get the queen to see she was tricked. That will take a little time."

"Time is very precious to me."

"You will have hundreds of years left and this time with family."

Harkin's face softened and he shifted in his chair. The silence hung in the air as the waitress came and put down two beers, smiling at Correk. Harkin let out a tired chuckle. "I see you have the family charm." He took a sip of the beer. "Family. I never thought I'd have another shot at that."

"Me either, but I've learned a few things from Leira. Family is more valuable than even this ring. You open up the world in between if that's what it takes to make it whole."

"I'm one rung down from the world in between."

"I'd say that's about right." Correk leaned forward on his elbows. "You send out a distress call to the Fixer just by wandering around. I knew where you were immediately. Someone here will know you and word will get back to Queen Saria. It's only a matter of time. Magicals down here could get hurt in the crossfire."

Harkin scowled, drumming his fingers. "Fine. I'll go back to the sanctuary after I finish the beer."

"Actually, when I saw where you were it gave me an idea. We're making one stop while we're down here. We're going to hide the ring where Wolfstan will never think to look."

"I thought it was safe with you."

"This is the backup plan in case something happens."

Harkin's voice grew loud and he growled, "Nothing will happen to you. I will kill him myself before I let that happen."

Wizards and witches shopping nearby turned to look at the ruckus.

"I can take care of myself and if I can't, there's Leira and Yumfuck." Correk saw the pain flash across Harkin's face and regretted saying it. "Show me how to open the ring." He held it out for Harkin.

"It's simple once you see how to do it." Harkin pushed magic through the ring and twisted and turned it in a series of quick motions, opening it up like a puzzle to reveal a miniaturized hard drive.

"Can Harkin complete his experiments with this?"

"He can at least get a helluva lot closer."

"Then we have to protect it as best we can. Let's go," he said, standing up and pushing back his chair. "I'm going to introduce you to the Jersey Willen."

Harkin closed the ring and got up reluctantly. "A Willen is going to do a better job of protecting what's in that ring?"

"This Willen can," said Correk, taking back the ring and securing it back in his pocket.

Harkin and Correk stood on the Jersey Willen's porch. It was listing to the right with chipped pots full of red geraniums all to one side. Correk knocked on the door and waited, the Willen pulling back a curtain to get a better look at who was there. His face brightened and his whiskers twitched as he worked at undoing the locks and opening the door a crack. "Is it just the two of you? That troll with you?"

"Yumfuck is topside. It's just me and... and my father." Correk stumbled over the word.

The Jersey Willen threw open the door, opening his arms wide. "Your father? Why didn't you say so? Hon,

Correk's brought his father," he called over his shoulder. "Do we have any of those week old cookies left?" The Willen hugged Harkin, quickly going through his pockets and drawing back a little disappointed holding a meager pile of pintas in his hand. "I feel like you need this more than I do," he said, giving them back.

"And this is who you want to trust with the most valuable thing I could give to you?"

"Valuable?" The Jersey Willen's eyes grew wider.

"Different kind of valuable," said Correk, "and very dangerous. Full disclosure, someone is hunting us trying to get to it. Someone powerful enough that we need to hide the ring down here with you." He held out the ring. "Will you personally keep it with you and show it to no one?"

The Willen's whiskers twitched and he rubbed his paws together nervously. "Violence makes me jumpy. Oh hell, for you Correk, I'll do it. Hand it over."

Harkin put his hand on Correk's arm. "You're sure?"

"Hey, never question the word of a Willen," said the Jersey Willen, agitated. "We may steal but we're no liars. If I give you my word, that's it," he said, brushing his hands together.

Harkin let go and Correk held out the ring. The Willen's paw brushed over his hand and the ring disappeared, buried in the folds of the Willen's skin. "Better than any safe," said the Willen. "Hell, I'll bet there's stuff in there I've forgotten about."

Correk smiled and shook the Willen's hand. "I'll be back for that when the danger has passed, but I don't know how long that will take." He gave a sidelong glance at his father, putting his hand on Harkin's shoulder. "If something happens to me, give the ring to my father, or to Leira. Those are the only two you trust with it. Understood?"

The Willen looked gravely at father and son. "Understood and I will carry out my mission," he said, making an X across his heart. "You can count on a Willen."

CHAPTER NINE

Yumfuck sat on the edge of his bed, dangling his little paws. "I miss Mara," he said, kicking the deck of Oriceran playing cards. "I miss Hagan." He flung himself backward, looking up at the ceiling. "I miss Texas." He rolled over, burying his face in the bedspread. "Calgon, take me away."

He pushed himself up and sat back, squaring his shoulders. "What would Hagan do?" He scratched his furry green head. "Eat something and then go look for a solution," he squeaked.

He put on his tiny navy blue backpack, his mask tied to one of the straps, and slid down the banister to the first floor, stopping in the front hall. He sniffed the air and wet a claw, holding it up. "They're nearby." Yumfuck opened the closet door and took another deep breath, smiling. "Come to me, my beauties." He burrowed past the boots piled up on the floor and found a stash of Cheetos hidden in one of Correk's tall boots. "Love this game. I win again. I'll just

81

take two, maybe three. Oooh, hey Twizzlers. Game changer."

A claw made neat work of the top of the bags and it wasn't long before they were all empty and the evidence stuffed under the couch in the living room. Yumfuck rubbed his belly and licked the orange dust off his fingers. "Correk really needs to up his hiding skills." He shook his little body and marched to the back door. "You can do this. There are friends to be made out there."

He pushed open the door and down the back steps, keeping close to the buildings, looking both ways and smelling the air. "This way." Yumfuck headed down the alley, turning at the side of the townhouse and making his way out to the sidewalk.

Hardly anyone was on the street in the middle of the day. "There has to be some action somewhere." He looked down the street and saw an elderly woman in jeans and a t-shirt, kneeling in front of her garden. She was digging around peonies in front of a large Federal style brownstone three doors down. She glanced up and down the street and leaned forward, pulling out a wand and blowing on the flowers, bringing them into full bloom.

"Magicals. Jackpot," whispered the troll. "Thank you for being a friend. Traveled down a road and back again," he sang quietly, pressing himself up against a picket fence and moving quickly toward the witch. He got closer and saw that her t-shirt read, *Sometimes I Wet My Plants*. "This could work," he whispered in delight.

Yumfuck edged up to her, gently tapping on her shoe. She wiped the sweat from her forehead and sat back, still on her knees, looking down at the smiling furry face looking up at her. "Two moons! A troll." She looked around furtively her silver hair fluttering in the wind. "Are you lost?"

"Kind of. I'm hoping a few friends will fix it." He stuck out a furry paw. "Yumfuck Tiberius Troll."

"You're an odd one, aren't you? Welcome to the neighborhood." She took his paw between two fingers and gave a gentle shake. "My name's Portia. I was born and raised in this world. My mother was from Oriceran and grew up near the Dark Forest in Virgo. I've lived here for the last thirty years." She looked at the troll slyly. "You're that troll from the internet. Haven't had that good a laugh in a while."

"If we could keep that on the QT. I took some heat for that."

"I'll bet. Magic out in the open like that. It's a wonder the Silver Griffins didn't come looking for you."

A ridge of fur went up along Yumfuck's back and he let out a shudder. "Trevilsom..." He shook his head. "Not the way I want to see Oriceran again."

"I take it you live close?"

Yumfuck pointed up the street. "Three doors away, the red brick one. I'm bonded with one of the Elves. Leira Berens."

Portia arched an eyebrow. "I've heard stories about her. A remarkable magical if the stories can be believed. You must be special too. She lives with a royal Light Elf, right?" She tilted her chin down. "You're in this neighborhood now? I hope that's good news." She held up her trowel. "Don't worry, I'm not asking for details. It'll be nice having you close by. A reminder of another home, especially for my husband."

"What are you planting?" He peered over her shoulder.

"A few things. Next are a few azalea bushes. The old ones died off during the last hard freeze."

"Azaleas..." Yumfuck tapped his chin. "You should try arie blooms from Oriceran. They last through all kinds of weather. They're a favorite of trolls."

"Hard to get and harder to explain." She sat back on her heels and brushed the dirt off her knees.

An older man walked out of the house carrying a tray with a pitcher, two glasses, and a plate of cookies.

"Portia, I brought you some..."

He stopped and did a doubletake, catching himself. "Marvelous! I heard a rumor there was a troll in the neighborhood."

"A *celebrity* troll, George. You were right! It's the rodeo-riding troll from the internet." Portia took Yumfuck's outstretched paw and got to her feet. "This is Yumfuck Tiberius Troll. He lives down the street now. This is George, my husband, a wizard."

"That's quite the name to live up to, Yumfuck. On several levels."

Portia held up her hand to the side of her face and whispered, "Everyone in this building is a magical of one kind or another. It's our version of a retirement co-op, with an added twist."

"Nice to meet you, George. Let me know if I can ever be of service. I do some protection and rescue work on the side."

"I get it...like a superhero."

Yumfuck lifted his chin, his hands on his hips, and puffed out his chest.

"Totally see it. You have a phone number, just in case? That'd be good to have." George carefully looked him up and down. "Would you like some lemonade? Portia made it."

Yumfuck let out a soft trill and took the glass, downing it in one gulp.

His lips puckered and his eyes grew bigger as he smiled.

"The wife makes it kind of strong." George chuckled. "Superhero work must make you thirsty."

"You get me, George. You really get me."

The door of the brownstone opened, and Portia smiled. "Oh, here come the others."

A group of seniors came slowly down the stairs. Yumfuck got up to help, but Portia put out her hand, stopping him. "Don't let them fool you. None of them are that old in magical years. It's all a show for any humans who may be watching. If we don't, then they'll think it's a remake of Cocoon over here."

"Look! A troll," said George. "Cut it out, Elijah, he's already bonded. That's Elijah, a Wood Elf. He has the place on the top floor. Can blend into damn near anything. Surprised me while I was trying to eat my Lucky Charms. Almost dropped the bowl."

"That was a good one." Elijah's glamour slipped for a moment. He touched the railing and his skin briefly took on the look of polished black iron, returning to a warm brown tone as the glamour was restored.

"Next time I'm throwing the bowl and asking questions later," said George.

"I'm Marcy and behind me is Emmitt. We're both Light Elves."

"That's most of the crowd," Portia said. She put up her hand and waved at the people making their way down the steps. "Emmitt come meet Yumfuck. He's our new neighbor."

"He's our new neighborhood watch with claws," said George, smiling.

"Would you look at that?" Marcy came closer, bending down, her hands on her hips. "I love trolls! Aren't you the cutest thing ever, and I like that name...has a certain ring to it. Never had the courage to try and bond with one..."

Yumfuck let out a cackle. "It's by mutual agreement, Marcy. You wouldn't have a chance."

Marcy shook with laughter, her bracelets jangling on her arm. "Too true."

Emmitt rubbed his bearded chin. "I saw you on a video. Well played, getting the locals to think it was all fake news." Emmitt pulled out a Payday candy bar and unwrapped it, the smell of salty peanuts hit the air.

Yumfuck swallowed hard and licked his lips, doing his best not to stare directly at it.

"Where are you guys off to?" Portia dug her trowel into the dirt and tossed a rock to the side.

Elijah shook his head. "We're heading down to the local Silver Griffins outpost to report our stolen lawn gnomes."

"My bike went missing last week," said Emmett. "They have so much going on over there we don't expect anyone to care."

"Hooligans." Yumfuck took another glance at the quickly-disappearing candy. "What were we saying?"

"We've all been here for decades," said Marcy, punching her fist into her hand. "It used to be the safest place you could be. There was a time when this was an up and coming neighborhood."

"Some of it got up and left." Elijah crossed his arms over his chest.

"Sad but true. Crime around here has skyrocketed. I've had to put stronger protections around this building every year. Not easy to maintain, either."

Yumfuck casually picked up a fallen peanut and popped it into his mouth as he formed a plan. This was his chance. *At last.* Robberies, muggings, and missing bikes and lawn gnomes.

"There's a lot of magic standing right here. How come you guys can't catch them? They had to leave a trail. Thank you, don't mind if I do." Yumfuck took a lemon cooler off the plate George held out to him and slid it into his mouth, trilling contentedly, powder dusting his belly. *Relief at last...*

George put the plate back on the tray. "This city is a wonderful place to live, but there are definitely sections you want to stay out of, even with a wand."

Elijah shuddered. "What he's trying to say is, not all magicals are law abiding. Magic is seeping back in and it's a whole new world out there."

"What about the Silver Griffins?"

"They do the best they can but they're going after bigger fish. Still, we're going to report it. Create a record, just in case."

Marcy looked at the townhouse down the block. "Do you live in that big house all on your own?"

"I have company. A family." The troll smiled, showing

his sharp little teeth. "Leira and my food pusher, Correk."
He laughed, holding his belly.

Portia smiled. "You are just what this neighborhood
needs."

"That and a good neighborhood doughnut place," said
Elijah.

"Aloha!" chirped the troll.

Marcy stood up. "Hey, are you guys hungry? I have mac
and cheese, and there's hot dogs left over from the cookout
yesterday. I can warm it up so it's ready when you get back
from the Silver Griffins precinct."

"I can help cook." Yumfuck put down his backpack.
Friends. This is going to be okay. He trilled softly.

"That'll work. Invite your roomies. I'm guessing they
have a little magic running through their veins, too? Good,
everybody come on over and we'll fire up the grill. It can be
a welcome party."

Yumfuck ran back to the townhouse but found it
empty. There was a note on the counter in Correk's neat
handwriting. *I know it's you. Leave me the KitKats.*

"There were KitKats? Challenge taken." The troll
glanced around the shelves in the pantry but didn't see
anything. *No time.* New friends and hot dogs were waiting.

He ran back out of the front door and down the sidewalk to where Marcy was waiting for him. He followed her
up the stairs to the second floor to her apartment.

"Where's your family?" she asked.

"Everyone's out. It's just me today."

"More than enough. We don't lock the doors much
during the day. The spell over this place has done a pretty
good job so far. I'm not even sure where I left my key."

Marcy shrugged. "I suppose that's going to be changing a little."

Yumfuck went in and looked around, picking up a snow globe of the Virgo mountains and pictures of the royal gardens and the Dark Forest on the walls. "These are all from Oriceran."

"Good eye. I like you. Anyone named *Yumfuck* has to have something special going on." Marcy moved a deck of cards with different Oriceran symbols on the backs, making room for some paper plates. Yumfuck gasped and clasped his hands to his chest in delight.

"I'll play you a hand." Yumfuck climbed on top of the counter. "I don't suppose you want to play for snacks?"

"You've seen these before?" Marcy picked them up, shuffling them in one hand. "My grandmother used them to tell people their future." Marcy gave Yumfuck a sly wink. "I use them to tell Emmett the future I want to see." She put them back down. "Maybe later. We have a party to throw!"

Marcy handed Yumfuck an orange ceramic bowl filled with Watergate salad. "It's a local favorite. More like dessert," she said, holding the bowl down to show him. Yumfuck leaned toward her with his tongue out but Marcy lifted the bowl with a laugh. "Is this too much for you to carry?"

Yumfuck held his hands over his head. "I'm freakishly strong. Eight feet of power packed into five inches. Hand it over."

"No sampling ahead of time." Marcy put the bowl in his hands, staying nearby and holding her breath. The five inch troll strutted across the kitchen floor, the bowl jiggling above him but never slipping. "I'll get the door," said Marcy, holding open the back door and pointing at the fire escape that led down into the fenced yard. "You sure you can make it down those steps?"

"With my eyes shut." He squeezed his eyes shut to demonstrate and jumped off the first step, the contents bouncing up and then back down into the bowl. He looked back at Marcy's pale face and winked. "See?"

Marcy opened her mouth to say something, but no words came out. Her fingers glowed for a moment, reaching out but she thought better of it. "It's just a bowl," she muttered. "Let him have his fun," she said, with one eye shut as she watched him bounce and jiggle off each step, letting out loud whoops of delight.

Yumfuck sucked in his cheeks and kept looking back. "What, whaaaaaat?" He inched toward the edge of the next step and jumped again. "Wooooohooooo!" The troll continued to bounce down the stairs, moving the bowl from left to right without losing a marshmallow.

Elijah was already out there heating up the grill, wearing a black apron that read, Classy, Sassy, and a Bit Smart-Assy. "Yumfuck! What do you have there?"

Marcy leaned over the railing. "Elijah? Is that you down there?"

"I stayed behind to help get the party started. No point all of us trooping down there so they can tell us nothing can be done." He put down the spatula and took the bowl from Yumfuck. "Ooooh Watergate salad. Dessert in a bowl but you get to call it salad. The best." Elijah scooped out a bowl for Yumfuck. "I'll get you a spoon." But he snorted with laughter when the troll dove in headfirst and was quickly at the bottom of the bowl.

Marcy came down the steps with small white bowls and spotted the peaks of whipped cream on Yumfuck's furry face. "First whipped cream?" She dished out a little more for him.

"First time mixing marshmallows with whipped cream," he said sticking his finger into his bowl. "Better than Cheetos." His eyes grew wider as he chomped down on a pistachio.

He dipped his paw, getting a marshmallow and pineapple on a claw with a glob of green whipped topping and shoved it into his mouth.

"That's high praise," said Marcy.

"We're back already." Portia and George came down the alley into the backyard. "An agent took the report, but that was about it," she said, her lips pressed together in a thin line.

"You never know," said Elijah. "We did our part. Time to party."

"Good, huh?" George asked, sitting down next to Yumfuck. "She makes it every summer and brings some over to me and Portia. Doesn't last two days."

Yumfuck climbed back in his bowl to lick it clean. He rolled on his back and put his furry little arms behind his head, letting out a deep breath. "Friends make a home."

"I couldn't have said it better." George held up a knuckle to fist bump with the troll.

"What's it like where you're from?" Elijah spread out the hotdogs on the grill. "I've heard stories about Oriceran, but I haven't had a chance to go. I keep meaning to take a trip, see the floating islands over the ocean. They have hotels?"

"Small cottages you can rent. It's all beautiful," Yumfuck

told him. "Blue skies, two moons, an endless forest filled with flowers and animals and birds. Thousands of trolls," he said, trilling. "Magical heaven."

"Do you have family there?"

"Yeah." Yumfuck smiled. "Hundreds of brothers and sisters. One of the smaller troll families."

"A few hundred..." George lifted an eyebrow. "I thought I would go crazy with three kids. Bless your mother."

"She's the best. There was the time she set up a treasure hunt and at the end were chocolate coins..."

Everyone took turns telling stories, welcoming the troll into the neighborhood and eating second and third helpings.

By the time night had fallen Yumfuck was full and happy. He curled up in George's golf hat while George, Elijah and Emmett play a rousing game of rummy with Marcy's enchanted cards. "Look at that! You will get a new bike," said George, slapping down a card.

Marcy stood at the base of the fire escape and yawned, giving the signal that the party was ending.

"*Wheel of Fortune* will be on in ten minutes," Portia yelled to George from their kitchen door at the bottom of the fire escape.

"That's my cue." George scooped the sleepy troll out of his hat and put it on his balding head. "It was a pleasure meeting you, Yumfuck. Don't be a stranger."

"Aloha." The troll smacked his lips and got up, slinging the backpack over his shoulders.

"Don't forget your leftovers, Yumfuck." Marcy came down the fire escape with a large covered paper plate. "A midnight snack for you."

He smiled and took the wrapped plate of leftovers from Marcy.

"I've heard about troll appetites." She gave a wave and held the back gate open for the troll. He yawned and held up the plate, bobbing down the alley toward home.

Just as he reached the Georgian townhouse a gust of cold wind swept around him, ruffling the fur down his back. He shivered, jiggling the plate, sensing something more than cold in the air. "It's just weather," he whispered. "Nothing more... I hope."

CHAPTER TEN

L eira stood at the edge of the dank tunnel, balancing her Merrill sneakers on the cobblestones set in place along the edge near the curved wall. A recent hard rain had flooded parts of the two hundred year old tunnel beneath Georgetown and left pools of water everywhere.

"Interesting place to meet. How did you even know this was here?"

"Sometimes even magicals like to go low tech," said Lois, smiling, pushing her glasses up her nose. She tapped her wand impatiently against her leg. "This tunnel was built by Silver Griffins back in the early nineteenth century and every year since then we add a little to the wards protecting it."

Up came her wand, thrust forward and shooting out a spray of fire that fizzled before it ever got to the wall. "You're standing in one of the soundest structures in this world. In recent years we've learned to tweak the wards and make it impossible to record audio or take pictures. Added bonus no one saw coming is you can't get cell coverage down here either." She slid her wand into a pocket. "I love this place."

Lois tilted her head to one side. "Not too many outside of the Silver Griffins ever gains knowledge of it, much less stand inside of it. But you said this was more important than Rhazdon and needed to be kept a secret. You got my attention."

"There's a new threat. A Light Elf named Wolfstan Humphrey. He's Oriceran born and now living in this world." Leira tapped her shirt covering the scar on her belly. "He's the force behind the mutilation of living things with artifacts and technology."

"Son of a bitch." Lois jabbed her glasses back up her nose again. "Wait till Earle hears this one. Boy, I'll tell you, when a magical goes bad there's no telling what will pop up." Lois stopped suddenly and eyed Leira. "Wait. That doesn't make *me* your go to. I'm not an expert on any of that kind of magic. What am I not seeing?"

Leira didn't hesitate to tell Lois the rest. An old Hagan rule. Don't spare others the bad news by waiting. It only makes it worse. "He runs a corporation, a large one, outside of Austin, Texas called Fleeker."

Lois gave an audible gasp. "Lily."

Leira waited, letting it sink in for Lois.

Lois shook her head, reflexively pulling her wand back out as if she was in a battle. "I know what you're asking. No and that's a hard no. That's my niece."

"I know what I'm asking, but the threat is overwhelming."

"Which is why you don't ask an untrained biologist to play spy for you with a monster who can..." She waved her wand in the air, throwing sparks at the large stones. "Who can create monsters. What if he caught her?" A shudder passed down her body.

"If I knew of another way, I would do it. I am doing it. All of them. He's had a long time to prepare whatever it is he's up to..."

"You don't even know?" Her voice rose, echoing in the tunnel.

"I have pieces of the puzzle but at this point trying to guess may cause me to miss details. He wants power and a lot of it, but what he plans to do with it is hard to say. We're not even sure what he would do with altered magicals if he ever manages to perfect the procedure." Leira licked her lips. "That's what he's doing on the tenth floor of the main building on the Fleeker campus. Yumfuck was able to get in there and saw it for himself."

"But that's impossible. Lily loves that place. She talks about it all the time like it's nirvana."

"That's the best way to hide a new address for hell."

Lois' eyes shined behind her glasses and she swallowed hard. "If you were asking me, I'd have already left for Austin. But my niece..."

"I'm sorry but I'm going to ask you to think about it. I have to because if we don't figure out a way to stop him, then hell will come right up to our doorstep, but it won't be on our timetable and Wolfstan Humphrey will be even better prepared. If we're going to fight him and win, it will take all of us working together."

"Come up with another way. Please."

"I will try." Leira took in a deep breath, letting it out

slowly. "This threat is growing every day and there's no time to waste."

"Can I tell Patsy?"

"You can even enlist her. You two make a dangerous team." Leira did her best to smile. "I believe we will be victorious in the end."

"How can you be so confident?"

"Because we have something Wolfstan doesn't and can't build with an artifact, a warm body and a mother board. We have each other and we are willing to put it all on the line as a team. That makes us stronger and we will prevail."

"But how many of us will live to see that day?"

"That is why we must work so hard now to cut him off at the knees before he gets an even bigger upper hand."

Lucius balanced his large frame on the small stool leaning over the genius bar. "I don't get it." He lifted the new iPhone higher in the air to smash it down, but the Apple Genius stopped him, gently taking the phone out of his hands.

"Okay, okay. We can walk through it again." The young man let out an exasperated breath and put a smile back on his face. "I know you can do this, Lucius. Sure, it's a lot. Every part of this world is new to you. Plus, it doesn't help that your fingers are so big." His smile was strained. "No offense."

"Careful, Jack." Lucius let out a low growl making the hair on the back of Jack's neck stand up.

"A little humor. Apparently, another more recent invention. Lucius, you said you wanted to be something that looked more like normal. I get it." He looked around, smiling at a coworker cruising past him with an iPad in a box. "Hey Phil," he said with a nod, leaning closer to Lucius and holding up the phone like he was showing him how to use the apps. "Okay, I don't have seven hundred years spent in goo, but I'm still a shifter in your pack. That makes me an outsider in this world and among magicals. But we can still blend in. Plus, these apps are pretty sweet." He tapped on a red app with a chili pepper sitting inside a yellow circle. "Look," he said, holding up the phone. "Recipes for days at your fingertips. Every variety. Even gives you a little history behind each one. Did you know that biscuits were invented in the eighteenth century? I would have thought they were older. Hey, we're not playing with the computers right now. Please focus, and don't bite me," Jack said sternly.

He swiped the screen to the left and tapped on a cartoon of piano keys. "Hey, what about Simply Piano? You can learn to play an instrument and get a hobby all at once. You need a hobby, dude. Warrior is way too old school. I appreciate that you stopped wearing the leather gear so much. Baby steps."

"Are you finished?"

"Just trying to help. Go ahead, try one for yourself."

Lucius grunted and tapped gently on the picture of a constellation.

"Sweet! Star Walk 2, good choice. Hey, I see that shifter in your eyes. No need." Jack pressed his lips together, waiting.

Lucius went back to looking at the app, his eyebrows

going up as he moved the phone around and the stars on the screen shifted, keeping up with his movements. "I wonder if they show Oriceran."

"Not yet, buddy, but that's a good idea for a startup among a select crowd. Try tapping on a constellation and see what happens. Right?" Jack nodded his head, satisfied. "See? Not so bad being part of this world. How about we buy this bad boy for you and then I'll get you lunch at California Pizza. You'll love it."

"We have a meeting tonight. The Dark Families are still a problem."

"All business, all the time. I suppose that's a good trait for our alpha. I know there's a meeting and I'll be there. But can we be something else right now? Two dudes hanging out. One with brand new technology in the palm of his very big hand."

Lucius hesitated, looking down at the twinkling stars in his hand and out the front window.

"Trouble is still going to be there later, Lucius. But if we can't have some fun in between the battles, what's the point? You survived all those years. It had to be for more than revenge. Hell, even the revenge part is done. Rhazdon is dead."

"I do like this app."

"Yeah, you do."

"Pizza on you?"

Jack grinned, patting his chest. "I got you. Then tonight we talk about protecting what's ours."

CHAPTER ELEVEN

Louie whistled as he walked down the sidewalk, maneuvering past people hustling in and out of doors, dressed in their best suits and tennis shoes as they made their way out for lunch.

"It's gonna be a nice night, Sam." Louie smiled, nodding his head at the skinny merchant selling purses, wallets, sunglasses, and movies in blank white cases.

"Morning, Louie." Sam held up a pair of aviator sunglasses and said in a deep, low voice. "Need anything today? Weather tomorrow should be sunny and clear."

"No, I still have the three pairs I bought off you."

"If it starts raining, come back. I'll have umbrellas. Just five dollars."

"Have to appreciate the hustle." Louie smiled, turning onto seventh street and heading for the familiar Chinese Friendship Archway that stood in front of Chinatown in the center of DC. "Home at last."

He made his way down the street, weaving in and out of the shoppers peering in windows and the locals sweeping off front steps. At eighth street he turned and went to the middle of the block, pulling open the door to the Two Lions restaurant. "After you, ladies," he said, smiling at the two middle aged women laughing and comparing their fortune on a small slip of paper.

"Mr. Hou," Louie called as he entered the restaurant. "Mr. Hou?" He walked by the red leather banquettes, stopping suddenly when a round man abruptly pushed out his chair to stand, going around the other side and winding his way through the table.

Mr. Hou came out of the kitchen, pushing the swinging door and wiping his hands on a towel hanging from his red apron.

"Evening Mr. Hou. My order ready?"

"It's not evening yet and the hostess at the front could have told you about your order."

"Not the same. I like our brief meetings." Louie followed him back into the kitchen.

"Louie, rent is due in five days."

Louie picked up the brown paper bag waiting for him on the metal counter. "Thanks Herman," he said, waving to the line cook. He left a twenty on the counter and put a clay salt cellar on top of it. "Left you a tip."

"Rent, Louie. Five days. A one bedroom in this neighborhood is highly desirable."

"I know, Mr. Hou, and you will have it," said Louie, "same as last month." He picked up his pace, heading toward the staircase in the back.

"No more cooking upstairs."

Louie spun around, smiling. "It was an honest mistake. I had no idea plastic would burn like that."

"That smoke cost me my lunch crowd."

"Again, very sorry. Takeout only. Seems like we both win." He turned around and kept moving.

"You need to start using the stairs in front, Louie. There's regulations about people wandering through the kitchen," yelled Mr. Hou, but Louie was already gone.

Louie took the stairs two at a time holding the warm bag closely. He stopped in front of his door and took out his wand, balancing the bag against his chest. He addressed each of the four locks, whispering incantations to remove the separate protection spells.

The door swung open and let him pass, closing and locking behind him again. He put the bag down on the short wooden counter and dropped his satchel on the slouching leather couch that came with the place. He sauntered over to the fridge that made up most of the tiny kitchen and was shoved into a corner and looked inside, his arm on top of the door. Two bottles of soda, a lime, a box of baking soda and a container of leftover dumplings. "Sweet, two sodas." He grabbed a bottle of Coke and perched on a barstool that wobbled to the right, leaning down to slide a Two Lions matchbook back under one of the legs.

"It's definitely not my cottage back on Oriceran, but it will do for now."

He rested the Coke on a glass case leaving a watery ring. Inside was a dried-up piece of tentacle Louie had found wrapped around the end of his boot from Dead Man's Walk.

The rest of the room contained an old pleather recliner, two side tables and a pine desk with one drawer. What sold him on the place was the wide-open space Louie used to practice with his sword.

Louie got up and set his perspiring Coke on the small end table next to the couch, grabbing the takeout and ripping open the bag, spreading it out over the counter. He pulled the lid off the hot and sour soup and breathed in the aroma. He dropped the lid and rubbed his hands together, picking up the plastic container and slurping in the soup. "Nectar of the gods," he muttered, licking his lips and slurping down more.

He pulled out an egg roll and bit off the end, wiping his greasy hands on a small white paper napkin and getting up to slide out a long wooden case from under the couch.

He sat back down and leaned back to grab his wand off the counter, tapping the lock and igniting sparks, still swallowing.

"Aperi mihi."

The lock glowed bright-blue and started to shake, clink, and clank, and with a shudder, fall open. Louie opened the case and stared at his sword. He rubbed his hands on his jeans and wrapped his hand around the hilt. A warm surge of energy coursed up his arm as he held the sword out in front, admiring the shimmering blade.

Begin. The sword was talking to him again, and he had learned it was in his best interests to listen. He took a wide stance and slowly swung the broadsword in loops to warm up. It was perfectly balanced in his hands, as if the ancient artifact was made for him.

Swing right, step with your left foot, jab, turn, swing low.

Louie followed the instructions, sliding back and forth

in front of the three windows that faced the street, ducking and pivoting, swinging the sword at a low height.

With every move, the sword instructed him further until he was able to repeat the pattern without a reminder.

Louie spun, raising the sword high, and sliced downward, stopping just inches from the worn rug under his feet. He was breathing heavily and wiped his forehead on the edge of his t-shirt.

His phone buzzed in his bag, drawing his attention from his practice. He straightened up, kissing the hilt of the sword and slid it into an old umbrella bucket by the couch.

He rifled through his bag and finally pulled out the burner phone Leira had given him, flipping it open to see a message from her.

Come to the house tomorrow morning. We need to talk.

"Okay." Louie wiggled his fingers to ready them to text back.

He pressed a few buttons to say, *no problem*, but autocorrect took over. "Fuck!" He jabbed at a button, a heart emoji popping up, and accidentally hit send. "That's going to be awkward. Shit... Will be there," he muttered, bent over the phone, typing carefully. "And send."

He turned the phone over in his hand and smiled, looking at the lights sparkling outside his window. "It's been a while since I've seen some action." He stretched his back, feeling an old familiar urge. "Time for an adventure to begin."

The smell of fried rice wafted up through the vents, making his stomach growl. "Maybe eat first." He stretched for the rest of the egg roll, eating the rest in one bite, his cheeks full. "Cooking for yourself is overrated."

Leira sat in the dark house in the red velvet chair, her feet propped up on the coffee table and the blue glow of the television barely illuminating the space. It was after midnight, but she couldn't relax. Yumfuck was curled up next to her, occasionally letting out gas from one end and then the other.

The television was prattling on, showing images of kitchens being redone and the owners shocked faces. Leira picked up the remote and muted it, leaning her head back against the couch.

"I wish Mom was here," she whispered.

Leira jumped as her phone rang and she sat up quickly. "Please let it be an informant."

The troll stirred, opening his eyes and smacking his lips, stretching out his arms and legs. "You get bored too easily."

"Go back to sleep," she said, answering the phone, looking at the screen.

"Mom..." she exclaimed.

"I felt your energy winding around me. You seemed lonely."

Leira sighed. "I couldn't sleep so I'm drowning my brain in infomercials."

"Did you know they make an all-in-one craft machine?"

Leira laughed, glancing at her screen. *Great minds...* "How is Don?"

"Oh, he's good. Sound asleep upstairs. But how are you? Why the distress signal?"

"I'm in that part of a case where waiting is the best answer."

"Ah, not your strong suit," said Eireka. "You get that from your grandmother. Where's Correk?"

"Out in some exotic land...or Wyoming...doing his Fixer duties," Leira replied. "I'm okay. Safe and sound, waiting to see how we attack Fleeker."

"How are Harkin and Correk getting along?"

"Better than I expected at this point."

"So, no one is trying to light up someone else anymore?"

"Nope, just that once. They actually can sit at a table. I think Correk really missed him. He's just not sure how to trust him yet. And without that it's hard for him to tell his dad."

"Let me say hello." Yumfuck's tiny paws were pulling at the phone.

"Mom... mom... okay fine but stop pulling." She picked up the troll and let him stand on her arm.

"Helloooooo Eireka." He pressed his face against the phone.

"It's not a cave," said Leira. She could hear her mother's laughter on the other end.

"Hello Yumfuck, I've missed you. Come and visit me soon."

"Make it FaceTime," he said to Leira.

"Go call her on your phone."

"I made some new friends, all magicals. You'd like them." His face was still pressed against the phone.

"Okay, show and tell is over. Let me talk too." Leira

scooped up the troll and set him in her lap. He picked up the remote and changed the channel till he found an old rerun of Cheers and unmuted it, cackling.

"I'm glad you have him," said Eireka, still laughing. There was an empty pause and her mother said, "Be careful out there. Wolfstan Humphrey is dangerous and has a lot to lose. Don't take anything about him for granted."

"Understood."

"Stay in touch and I'll call to check on you. Well, I am going to shut it down and get some sleep. I just wanted to check and make sure you were okay."

"Yes, go. Don't worry about me. You *are* a newlywed, after all. There must be more exciting things for you to do."

"Nothing more important than my daughter," her mom replied. "Love you more."

"Love you most," Leira replied, hanging up.

She tossed the phone onto the couch and put the troll back down, standing up and walking over to the window. She shoved her hands in her pockets and felt the magical key to Turner's hidden sanctum. She put her hands on her hips and lifted her chin. "Time for a late night run and see the neighborhood from a different perspective."

"You say something?" Yumfuck didn't wait for an answer and rolled backward with laughter, still holding the remote.

"Never mind and leave Correk's stash alone while I'm gone."

The troll hiccuped and let out a cackle.

Leira changed her clothes and grabbed a water bottle, heading out the door and stopped at the bottom of her stairs, taking in a deep breath and bending over to touch her toes. The streets were quiet except for music filtering over from the bars on Nineteenth Street.

The door of the townhouse next to hers opened and a young woman stepped out, dragging a large white plastic bag of trash. "Damn, I thought these things weren't supposed to tear." She tilted the bag, so the tear was on top, holding it away from her cropped jeans and blue Keds and started down the front steps.

"Oh hey!" The woman's face brightened when she saw Leira standing under the streetlight. "You're the new neighbor." She left the bag flopped over at the bottom of her stairs and rushed over, wiping her hand on her jeans. "I'm Angel, Angel Moss. I live right next door to you with my husband, Matt."

Leira shifted the water bottle and shook her hand, glancing down the sidewalk. She was itching to run. "I'm Leira Berens and I live there with my... my boyfriend, Correk." She felt her face warming and stepped out of the light.

"We saw you moving in and I've been meaning to bake something and come over to say hello. Of course, first I'd have to learn how to bake. Oh, wait right here." She held up her hands, walking backward, smiling until she got to the steps and turned, running up them.

Leira looked down the block again, and back up at the neighbor's house debating the degree of rude if she just took off running. She opted for stretching her hamstring, pressing her foot against the step, instead. "Time to make some new friends, I guess."

Angel came out her door, still talking and carrying a six pack of beer with the logo, Three Stars Brewing and a skull and roses on the side. "I don't know my way around most of the kitchen, but I know my beer. A housewarming present from the Moss' to you and..."

"Correk and thank you," said Leira putting the beer under her arm.

"It's local and some of the best. Have you found your way around the town yet? I can help you out with a few restaurant suggestions and who delivers here. Ordering out is another one of my strong points."

"Yeah, yeah that would be great." The beer felt cold against her skin and she found herself smiling, watching Angel chatter away, pointing down the street in one direction. "The duckpin bowling at the Eleanor is the best but maybe that's because of the Rueben and bloody Mary I got there. Matt loves to bowl but he has to bring his own bowling shoes. He's weird about wearing communal shoes." And then pointing over Leira's head. "The Eastern Market over by the Capitol is where you want to get your produce when the weather is warm, and they'll have a flea market too. I furnished a lot of this place digging through flea markets."

She's a wall of sound. An entire bar of regulars in one small body. Leira put the beer on her front stoop behind a potted plant, still listening to Angel.

"Of course, we'll have to take you and Correk to Blues Alley for music. You actually have to go down the alley to get to it. And that's not far from the Exorcist steps. If we all drink enough at Blues Alley we can try running up and down the stairs. I slipped once and slid down the whole thing on my ass. Never felt it till the next day."

Fuck, I actually like her. She hasn't grilled me about anything. Not once.

"Hey, what are you two doing this Friday? Matt and I can take you to the Blue Duck Tavern. All locally sourced. You'll love it!"

"Sure!" Leira blurted it out, surprising herself.

"Yeah? Oh great, we can practically walk there. It's a few blocks but it looks like you're a runner and I saw that handsome partner of yours and he can probably handle a walk. Maybe we can meet over here first and go from there." She grabbed Leira in a tight hug before Leira knew what to do, squeezing even tighter. "A new friend!" said Angel, letting go to step back, a wide grin on her face.

Leira felt an ache she didn't know was there easing just a little. *A new friend.* She gave a crooked smile, blinking and said, "We'll be there. Yeah, and I love bowling. I was on a team in Austin." *Estelle would not recognize me right about now. But she'd like it.* Leira smiled again.

Leira put the beer inside the fridge and headed back outside. She ran for almost an hour, turning onto eighteenth street and running past the World Bank, blocks from the lights of the White House. She finally slowed down to a jog, sipping water and listening to the sound of a dog barking in the distance.

She slowed to a walk in front of a red brick house shaped like an octagon with a brick center that curved outward and a balcony on the second floor. She took another sip, balancing her toes on a curb and stretching her ankles, admiring the old house.

"Neeeevvvveeeerrrr!" A woman's scream from the house ripped through the quiet night from inside the house. Leira didn't hesitate, dropping her water bottle by the side of the stone steps and running to the door, jiggling the handle. Locked tight.

"Neeeevvveeerrrr!" The scream rang out again.

"Fuck me, I'm coming in." She pulled in energy through her feet and set out an intention. "Open up the door and show me where she is." The stream of glittering magic went out ahead of her, rolling through the lock and moving the tumblers. The door clicked open and Leira pushed inside, chasing the energy.

"Neeeevvveeerrrr!" A chill went down her spine and she ran up the curved staircase, footprints left behind in the dust, bursting into a bedroom and stopping cold. The trail ended in an empty bedroom. No one was there.

"Hello?" Leira ran to the closet, pulling open the door, her eyes glowing and her palm itching to make a fireball. "No one." She stepped back out into the room, standing still and listening.

The air in front of her shimmered, a bubble hanging in the air, growing larger and pushing toward her. Leira leaned away from it, a cold air blowing against her face. The bubble grew and hands appeared on the other side, pushing toward her. A woman's face pressed against the bubble and she opened her mouth and screamed, "Neeeevvveeeerrrr!"

"The world in between," gasped Leira. "This is a thin place between the worlds." Leira's muscles were tense as she moved closer, watching the woman desperately look for a way to push through to the other side.

Leira pressed her hands against the bubble, the chill spreading up her wrists, unable to reach the woman. "I'm sorry," she quietly said, watching the woman writhe and suddenly be sucked backward, rapidly disappearing from view.

The bubble shrank till it disappeared and Leira was left standing in the room, her chest moving up and down and her heart beating faster. She waited a moment and turned, running back down the stairs and out the door, pulling it closed behind her.

She grabbed her water bottle and looked up at the address. *Seventeen-ninety-nine New York Avenue.* "I will be back," she whispered. She ran toward home and was almost there when she realized something was different. The dark mist had not reached out to her this time. Still, she couldn't shake the feeling that something was off.

The feeling got stronger and she picked up her pace, taking a quick left at the next corner and ducking down a long alley. She slowed down toward the other end, scanning both sides for any sign of movement.

A feral cat's meowing and hissing startled her, and she tripped and fell backward onto her ass.

"Oomph." She rolled over and quickly pushed back to her feet, brushing the gravel off her hands. *Someone is following me. I know it.*

Holding on to her water bottle, Leira spread her feet apart and breathed deeply. She pulled the energy from the ground and up through her center, the scar on her belly warming. Her eyes glowed as symbols slowly flipped and turned on her skin, gradually picking up the pace. She closed her eyes and set an intention.

Find nearby magic trails. Streams of sparkling light appeared, floating in different directions, crossing each other. Evidence of different magicals walking past at various times during the day. It was appearing like a movie playing in her head.

Leira focused on any recent trails, digging underneath the layers.

Crash!

A glass bottle shattered in the nearby alley and a man groaned. A millennial in a suit and tie was backing up, his eyes wide. "You... how did you... your eyes were glowing... what the fuck..." The words sputtered out of him.

"Never was, never will be."

He froze in place giving Leira enough time to grab her water bottle and jog out of the alley, turning the corner and running the rest of the way home. Still, she couldn't shake the feeling someone was watching her most of the way.

CHAPTER TWELVE

"I'll do the Kung Po Chicken with fried rice, fried wontons, eggrolls, and give me a small order of shrimp fried rice for a friend." Louie leaned on the counter at the Two Lions.

"Louie!" Mr. Hou waved his hands in the air excitedly. "What is up?"

"I see you got my check. Look..." Louie held out his hands. "I'm picking up the food at the front."

Mr. Hou held up his fist, waiting for Louie. "Yeah, sure. Local customs." He completed the fist bump and smiled.

"Louie gets the family discount," he said, wiping his hand on his stained apron. "Family. He is family. Egg rolls half price!"

"We're doing a one eighty with this bromance. Nothing like a discounted egg roll. Thank you, Mr. Hou."

"Are you going out to search for more junk?" Mr. Hou waved to a waiter, pointing to a table waiting for water.

"Artifacts. Valuable artifacts. Like junk but worth something. Not today Mr. Hou." Ava Hou, the owner's daughter

MARTHA CARR & MICHAEL ANDERLE

came out of the kitchen and wove her way to the front, dropping the bag next to Louie. She kissed her father on his cheek and winked at Louie, picking up empty plates as she headed back to the kitchen.

Louie reached in the bag and pulled out a wonton, popping it in his mouth and handing the girl a twenty dollar bill. "I've got to get going, Mr. Hou," said Louie, distracted and watching Ava walk away as he chewed

"When you come back tonight, I will give you some of the leftover dumplings. No charge."

"You," Louie fist bumped him again, "are a great landlord."

Louie grabbed his bag and headed out the door, turning left onto Sixth street toward the Gallery Place stop.

He went down the steep escalator, following the steadily moving crowd and inserting his Metro card, grabbing it back as he pushed through the turnstile.

The subway car was already there, and Louie ran the last few steps, jumping through the doors as the familiar bell dinged overhead. "Doors closing."

He found an empty seat in the back, facing the row of people and sat down, putting his bag on his lap. His stomach gurgled and he slid a wonton out, pushing the whole thing in his mouth.

"Ahem."

Louie froze as a woman sitting on a bench facing the center cleared her throat. He looked up and recognized the magical energy surrounding her. *Fuck! A witch. Please don't be a Silver Griffin.* "Shouldn't you be looking for a Starbucks?"

The woman harrumphed, straightening her suit jacket

and sitting up straighter. She brushed back a stand against her stiff blonde helmet of hair. She tapped a sign hanging just behind her that read, "NO EATING," and raised her eyebrows. Louie sighed and closed the bag, not wanting to make her look at him any more closely. He was still wanted by some Silver Griffins for a little unresolved matter.

She narrowed her eyes at him, and he noted the handle of her wand sticking out of her large purse that had cats embroidered on the outside.

"All right," Louie said, putting his hands in the air. "I can wait, but when I have to eat cold Chinese, I'm blaming you."

She snorted and looked back down at her phone.

Louie leaned back in his seat, opening the bag and taking a long whiff. The witch looked up with a scowl.

"There's nothing up there about smells, lady."

Leira wiped her hands on the towel and looked up at the sound of pebbles hitting the back door. She opened the door and found Louie with a bag cradled in the nook of his arm, chewing and tossing pebbles at the same time.

"Louie, you made it."

"Nice set of wards you have on the place. I tried a few things and found myself back down the alley on one of them. Turner Underwood teach you those?"

"Some of them. Jackson taught me some too."

"I don't know if I should be jealous that I've known him longer and he's never shown me anything like that." He put the bag down on the table, pulling out the cartons and opening them up. "You have a fork? I don't need a plate. Conservation in everything."

Leira got out a fork and handed it to him. "You're a deep well, Louie."

Yumfuck came sliding down the banister standing up, wearing his backpack. He came bouncing into the kitchen, inhaling deeply.

"Mmmm, shrimp fried rice!" Yumfuck tilted back a carton, pouring food in his mouth.

"Thought you might want to have lunch with me." Louie smiled and ruffled the green fur on his head.

"On my way out," Yumfuck told him, his cheeks full.

"In a while crocodile."

"See you later, instigator," said the troll, heading out the back door.

Leira snorted. "That does seem about right."

"No problem," he called over his shoulder as Yumfuck shut the front door behind him.

"Let's sit in the living room." Leira waved over her shoulder.

"Can I bring the food?" Louie shook his head. "I've been shrimp blocked all morning."

"Yeah, there's nothing in here you can hurt."

Leira sat down in the red velvet chair and crossed her legs. Louie followed her and sat on the couch, pulling the coffee table toward him and lining up the cartons.

"I like what you've done with the place," he told her. "A bit bigger than mine, but just as early rundown and extremely not modern."

"Thanks, it's home." Leira wrinkled her nose, watching him shovel food into his mouth.

"Couldn't eat on the train and I was starving. It's amazing how many rules this world has. Don't steal there, don't eat here." Pieces of rice were falling onto his shirt when he glanced up and saw Leira, one eyebrow arched. "Growing wizard. Hey, where's Correk?"

"Out playing Fixer. Finish chewing. I have an adventure for you."

"You make it sound like you're doing me a favor. You say adventure, but you mean scary, deadly, maybe involving monsters kind of mission."

"I need you to locate Sirius," Leira said, looking him in the eye. "He set a pretty good trap for me recently and it got a little too dicey. But the worst of it, he was actually the bit player. Someone else was manipulating him."

"Sirius is someone else's bitch. Whoa. That is deep."

"Use those expertly tuned tracking skills and find Sirius for me. If we can pull him out of the mix, we may be able to destabilize an even greater foe."

"I'm on it... as soon as I finish this," he said, taking another bite of food.

"Priorities, I get it. I can even pack you snacks for the road. I know where there are KitKats."

"Now you're talking."

Correk opened a portal onto the expansive lawn that over-looked the lake in Austin. Turner Underwood was down by the water, his hands behind his back. His cane was up on the patio, leaning against one of the Adirondack chairs.

"I got your summons." Correk came and stood next to

him, watching a large mouth bass break the surface and flop back into the water.

"I have this theory based on hundreds of years of observation." Turner squinted his eyes against the sunlight bouncing off the lake.

"Okay, we're coming at a problem sideways. I'm listening."

"Family is the best thing that can happen to any living being. It doesn't matter what kind of species." A sudden breeze ruffled his hair. "And it's the worst because when things don't go well, we can't just pack up and go."

"We're talking about Harkin now, aren't we?"

Turner patted Correk on the shoulder and started to trudge up the sloping lawn to the patio and his chair. "Harkin has not been cooperating lately. He is his own worst enemy."

"I'm very familiar with that part of his personality." Correk followed him up the hill, the heels of his boots sinking into the soft ground. "He barrels forward trying to do the right thing and when it doesn't turn out, he barrels forward again trying to fix it."

"Funny that you chose a mate with the same trait but better judgment." Turner settled into one of the Adirondack chairs with a grunt.

"He's not going to stay put for long. Mostly because we all want him to do it. He'll try to help eventually."

"Sit, Correk. There's a solution to all of this. Do you want any coffee? Two Fixers should be able to come up with something interesting." Turner made a steeple on his belly with his hands. "It will take a confession from Wolfstan Humphrey to clear your father of Fraekin's murder. Queen Saria won't accept anything less."

"Wolfstan is far too cagey to confess to any of us about anything."

"True, but he has an ego that has to be fed by somebody. Probably not someone he can trust. I doubt that person exists on either world. But instead someone he thinks is under his control that he could destroy at a moment's notice."

"Who would want that mission?"

"That is the piece of the solution that we still need to find. I had hoped that Lily Sharpton would help, but Lois has a point. Lily is untrained and might not last long up against Wolfstan." Turner pushed himself out of the chair, grabbing his cane and tapping it on the slate as he headed toward the house. "I'm suddenly hungry for a burrito. Come keep me company before you run off to save another misguided magical."

CHAPTER THIRTEEN

Lily Sharpton sat on the edge of the metal folding chair in the town hall meeting at Fleeker headquarters. Ed Shifford, the CFO had come out in his lime green polyester jacket signaling another record earnings quarter for the company. Annual bonuses were assured and there was talk of new jobs opening up. Everyone in the large auditorium that served more often as a cafeteria, was smiling and laughing at all of Ed's jokes. "Money isn't everything, but it definitely keeps you in touch with your children." A hearty laugh rose from the crowd along with a smattering of applause.

Screens were set up near the front that showed gatherings at other company locations and their reactions. Everyone was enjoying themselves.

Lily chuckled, glancing at her coworker, Phyllis as she took a sip of her coffee. "I love working here," she muttered.

Wolfstan Humphrey came striding onto the small platform, clapping and smiling as Ed took a bow and headed off the other side. "Thank you, Ed, for looking after all the dollars and cents for us." He waved to the crowd which began clapping louder, waving again with his lips pressed together to signal to the rank and file to settle down.

"We've got a lot to get to on today's agenda. First we have a few employees we would like to recognize."

"Oh damn!" Lily's supervisor, Ray Jenkins was nervously flipping through the papers in his leather briefcase. He looked up, sweat already forming on his forehead, searching every face close to him. "Lily! Oh, thank God. I forgot the certificates. We're the last group. Can you run back and get them? I left them in my office. They should be right on my desk. Here, use my key card. It'll be okay."

Phyllis' eyes grew wide and she looked away at the mention of the key card. It was against the rules to even touch someone else's card and they were to be used only when the sub-derma chip failed. Lily hesitated, but Ray shoved the card at her. "Here, here! Go, go! If I don't have them by the time Mr. Humphrey calls those names heads will roll. Go!" He waved frantically at her, too low for anyone up front to see, patting his face dry with a napkin.

Lily carefully slid out of the row, stepping over feet and muttering an apology after stepping on someone's Florsheims. She walked as quickly as she dared toward the exit, not looking back and pushed the swinging door gently, opening it just enough to slide through to the broad hallway. Then she started running for the elevator.

Lily jabbed the button a few times, considering and then quickly discarding the idea of using a little magic to get the elevator to arrive faster. "Yes!" There was a soft ding and the doors immediately opened as Lily leapt forward, scanning the executive key card and hitting the button for the top floor. It was all adding more excitement to her day. She had never been up on the top floor, much less unsupervised.

The elevator rose with a whoosh, speeding past the lower floors and coming to a sudden stop at the twelfth floor, the doors finally opening after a few moments. It all felt like it was taking forever.

Lily stepped off the elevator and felt the blood rush to her head. "Crap. Which office is his?" Her heart was beating faster, and her face was warming as she tried to figure out which office looked like a mid-level vice president. She ran into the first office she saw and scanned the papers on top of the desk. There were folders stacked on the corner of the desk about upcoming projects. "Nope, this isn't you, Ray."

She ducked out, hoping no one would see her running in and out of each office, and tried a few more. "Where the fuck did they put you Ray?" She could feel the time slipping away. "No one will ever know. Maybe." Lily pulled out her wand and whispered fervently, "Finders keepers." She swore, waving her wand to try and start over. "That's not the right one. Nothing was taken. Where there are..." She stopped the spell mid-sentence. A twinkle of light was already drifting away from the wand, wandering down a private hall and into the largest office.

Curiosity got the best of her and Lily followed in its wake, glancing over her shoulder. "If this is your office, Ray, I have seriously underestimated you." The spark circled over the large desk in the center of the room, slipping into a drawer on the right near the bottom, spinning around in the lock with a *tick, tick, clink*.

"On top my ass, Ray. Oh geez." The shallow drawer slid open easily but instead of papers, all Lily found was a necklace with a round gold circle engraved with the royal Oriceran seal. Lily felt a chill go down her back and shuddered, picking up the necklace and holding it up to the light. Along the back were deep red dots of dried blood still clinging to it. On the other side of the circle the name, Fraekin was etched in script.

Lily swallowed hard and slipped the necklace in her pocket, sliding the drawer shut. She straightened up and pushed a few papers around on the desk to confirm whose office it was, but she already knew. "Wolfstan Humphrey... what have you done?"

She backed her way out of the office, making circles with her wand. "Never here, never there." The trail of magic she had created fractured into small pieces, rolling along the carpeted floor and sliding into the cracks. The color was drained from Lily Sharpton's face as she walked quickly to the next office, finally locating the certificates, and running to the elevator, not looking back.

CHAPTER FOURTEEN

The large ballroom was silent. A row of young wizards and witches stood against the walls, not even looking at each other.

Toby Wheeler pressed his hands against the wall, leaning forward to get a better look at some of the late arrivals. "Eyes forward," barked a husky wizard walking past them.

In the center of the room the heads of all the old Dark Families were taking their seats around the long, wide table. Banners fluttered over their heads with the different family crests.

Oversized wizards stood at every entrance, their wands poised to quell any threat or annoyance.

The main doors shuddered and opened as the room grew tense. Toby leaned forward again, peering around the wizard on his left but the young witch on his other side dug her nail into the soft spot of his shoulder, giving him a menacing look. "I'm not getting noticed today for the wrong reasons," she hissed. "I have big plans."

Agnes walked in holding her head up, nodding to Philomena and Jackard, two matriarchs from the western region seated at the top of the table.

"Where's Sirius?" whispered Toby, still looking behind Agnes even as the doors were closing.

The young witch, Isabel, rolled her eyes, tucking a blonde curl behind her ear. "How can you be so clueless and still breathing in this family?" she asked in a low voice. "He disappeared a couple months ago after the shifters got away. No one's seen him since."

"I wish I could have disappeared."

"I could still help you with that wish."

Toby did his best to scowl at her, but she smirked and leaned back against the wall.

"Women," he muttered. "They're all some kind of witch."

A bulky wizard growled at Toby and Toby's eyes widened as he pressed his lips together.

Agnes came and stood at the head of the table, placing her hands flat on the table. "Extemporius!" She flung an arm in the air, sealing the room from outsiders.

"Agnes, you're breaking protocol with this meeting. We had decided to wait till Sirius surfaced," said Jackard, her dark hair pulled back in an intricate bun at the nape of her neck. Holding it in place was a gold clasp in the shape of the infinity sign.

Agnes drew herself up, stiffening her back, her long blonde hair shifting along her back. "Sirius has been gone long enough. No one has heard from him and we are losing time." Her face twitched at the lie. *Let Wolfstan have him.* "There are certain obstacles to maintaining our rightful place in this world." *I will make a better deal.* "The greatest aggravation is still Leira Berens." The last words came out through gritted teeth.

She smoothed an eyebrow, collecting herself and remained standing over everyone seated at the table. "That has proven to be more difficult than we expected. But we have a new ally in Wolfstan Humphrey..."

"He's just an Elf," a wizard blurted, slouching back in his chair. "We don't canoodle with Elves."

"The powerful enemy of my enemy is a friend willing to snuff out a Jasper Elf. He has the means to do it. We will help him."

"What if Sirius returns in the middle of your new plans?" Philomena dragged a deep red nail along the top of the table leaving a barely perceptible scratch.

"A problem for another day."

"And your thoughts on who his successor should be?" asked Jackard, her eyes hooded.

"Stop baiting me, Jackard," said Agnes, tapping the end of her wand on the table. "You'll find I have a line just as deep and scarred as Sirius that no one should cross." She licked her shiny pink lip. "That brings us to the shifters."

A murmur floated through the room and several at the long table shifted in their seats. The corners of Agnes' mouth curled ever so slightly. She snapped her fingers, a blue spark igniting and a wave of static electricity pulsed out, jolting everyone into silence. "It's true, our plan for the shifters failed. Failed miserably." The memories of Juliana's death still haunted Agnes. "But this is a new day and we have a new plan." She gestured to a group of young witches and wizards against the wall, including the young witch next to Toby.

"Come here, this is your moment. Come, come."

"What do you expect these children can accomplish that we could not?" Jackard snapped at the closest young wizard, making him startle and step back. She smiled, satisfied, draping an arm over the back of her chair. "Lucius will eat them for lunch. Crunch your bones, suck out the marrow."

"Enough, Jackard. They're all family. They can practice by hunting shifters in Lucius' pack and they'll get better at it. One shifter at a time."

"His pack is organized and hunts together. I'm guessing you see a few of our younger cousins as necessary collateral damage?"

"They've been training," Agnes said raising her voice. "You were asked to help them train, Jackard, but were far too busy. Question my place at the head of the family again. Throw doubts on my plans," growled Agnes.

"Cousin." A wizard who had been sitting at the far end quietly listening, stood up.

"Franco, you have something to add?" Agnes waved the back of her hand at the young group, moving them back to their positions along the wall.

"If I may? I believe we are all concerned that things are spinning in circles and not moving forward." He drew a circle in the air with his finger.

"And you have a different plan?" Agnes held her breath, staring him down. She needed to inflict some fear in the others, or her reign would be abruptly and violently cut short.

"All of our focus should be on eliminating Leira Berens," said Franco, looking half bored. It was all Agnes could do not to roll her eyes.

"Keep banging your head against that wall, Franco. I'll do my best to shed a tear at your funeral when she's had enough."

"I put my money on Agnes," Isabel whispered to Toby. "I see a fire in her that is ready to blow. I think she would help the witches rise amongst the ranks again."

Toby chuckled. "I put my money on Franco."

"The bored wizard?"

"He's been around since the invention of the locomotive and has been in his share of battles." He leaned closer, a shudder passing through him at the memory of the fire. "On top of that, Agnes lost her library. All of her oldest spell books are gone."

"She lost one library. There's always been rumors that Sirius kept a second library curated with the oldest magic."

"You're putting children in charge of hunting fur and fangs that even Juliana couldn't stop," said Philomena. Others at the table started to voice their concerns, one talking louder than the next.

"Enough!" Agnes shouted down the other elders. "All in favor of my plan, raise your wands," she said, tapping her wand in the palm of her hand. "We don't have time to stand around and argue."

Toby watched, barely able to take in a deep breath, wondering if mayhem would break out. The elders voted, all but Philomena and Franco lifting their wands, which silenced the room. Agnes straightened her cream-colored Chanel jacket and finally sat down, clearing her throat.

"Wolfstan Humphrey wants to get rid of Leira Berens even more than we do, if that's possible. He is asking for our help."

"You mean demanding at the end of a sword." Franco shrugged. "He reminds me of a younger me. We let him in, there will be no getting rid of him."

Agnes smiled. "We have been friends for too long, haven't we Franco. Do we want another enemy who is just as dangerous? Or do we want to take a chance that this Wolfstan can finally take out our greatest threat?"

"What exactly does he want from us?" asked Jackard. "Someone like that will have a very high price."

"He wants a seat at this table." Agnes kept a stony expression, her hand lightly resting on her wand.

Franco sat up straight, leaning across the table toward Agnes. "You want to give an Elf who was once in Trevilsom Prison a seat at the Dark Families table? Next we'll be hanging his banner overhead."

Philomena's eyes narrowed and she tilted her head, looking at Agnes. "What exactly did he threaten you with? You would never even consider it without a good enough reason. It's either power or death and I don't see Wolfstan sharing his power."

"Did he threaten all of us," said Franco with a leering smile. "Does he think he can wipe out all of us?" he asked, waving an arm at the assembly. "This is only a small portion of our numbers."

Agnes swallowed hard to settle her stomach. Wolfstan had made a point to show her the mechanics of what happened on the tenth floor. "I got a personal tour from

Mr. Wolfstan of his operations in Texas. I've seen what he's working on with magicals and trust me, if he pulls any of it off, death would be a blessing. Better we stay close to him on his good side and stay out of his experiments. Then, when the opportunity presents itself and he's rid us of that damn Jasper Elf, we will find his vulnerable underbelly and destroy him and that damnable Fleeker machine."

Leira ran her hand along the broad side of the sword, admiring its balance. "This entire thing must be an artifact. I wonder what it does." The white stone on the handle shimmered and swirled just below the crest of Oriceran forged into the hilt. "Correk... Correk?" She glanced over her shoulder and realized Correk was still back in the room with the fireworks.

She tried to step into the hallway with the sword but was shoved back by a protection spell. The sword tugged at her hand. "Okay, I get it. No wandering off with any weapons of a lot of mass destruction." Leira carefully put the sword back on the wooden pegs holding it in place and shut the case, trying again to go back into the hallway. This time the ward let her pass.

"Correk? You're missing some pretty good stuff."

The Light Elf came wandering out of the room, still looking back over his shoulder, his mouth hanging open.

Leira let out a sigh, her forehead wrinkled. "Surely in all the years you've lived you've seen fireworks before. Hell, you've probably seen them in battles."

"I changed it to High Noon. Did you know there's Wi-Fi in there?"

"And a snack station." Leira grabbed Correk by the arm before he could turn back. "You do get that we can buy our own."

"Yumfuck's been eating all of mine. I found tiny claw marks." He shook his head. "I've even tried a glamour on the last stash and he broke through."

"You bothered with a glamour on your Little Debbie's? We may need an intervention. I mean, I'd understand if we were talking bacon." She pulled him down the hallway. "There are rooms that will make that look kind of sedate. Just wait."

"What's in there?" Correk peered inside the weapons room.

"Lots of potential destruction. It seems kind of cool till you get to what comes next. Come on, we can look at those later. We are supposed to meet the Moss' in front of our house by seven. We don't have all day."

"A double date. You're sure this is a good idea? You didn't even meet the husband."

"It's a great idea. We need to do more normal things instead of always blowing shit up."

"It seems so... human."

"You can do it big guy. I believe in you. This is going to be a great day. I can feel it. First this magical wonderland and then we actually make some new friends and go out like a couple. Wait till you see what's behind door number three."

"You're sure you're not overselling..."

"That's what I said, and no," she said, wiggling her eyebrows and getting a laugh out of Correk.

"Pretty confident, Berens."

Leira gave him a crooked smile, pulling him into the room just beyond the armory. She pulled him close, turning around with her back to him and his hands at her waist as a single bubble formed around them. "Prepare to have your mind blown."

She pushed at the doors and they exited the bubble, entering into the endless room. Correk worked his jaw as his ears popped from the change in air pressure. He looked up, pulling Leira closer against his chest, watching a school of red and silver flowerhorn fish dart past them. A fever of stingrays swam overhead, gracefully pushing through the water.

Leira breathed in deeply, slowly letting out air and leaned back against Correk. "We could take staycations in just this room."

"Decompress from battles."

"That's a dark thought. Hey, that's new." Leira leaned forward, watching a mermaid swim closer, coming to the bottom to wave at them. On her wrist was a bracelet with an S and a G intertwined. The mermaid smiled and gave Leira a thumbs up, swimming away, her tail moving up and down in the water as she swam in the wake of a blue marlin.

"Turner Underwood has so many alliances and secrets. Do you think that's what you'll be like some day?"

Correk kissed the top of Leira's head. "How do you know that's not me already?"

"Because you talk in your sleep. A lot." She turned

around and kissed him, her tongue searching inside his mouth. "Do you think there are cameras in here?"

Correk laughed, "I thought you said there was even better things to see."

"They can wait. I have something to show you right here."

CHAPTER FIFTEEN

"I think I can count on one hand the number of times I've seen you in a dress. It usually takes a mission or a wedding." Correk held onto Leira's hand as she took a short spin on the sidewalk in front of their house. She was dressed in a short orange dress covered in eyelets. "I kind of like it," he said.

"You clean up pretty well yourself. You're actually wearing a shirt with buttons. Cowboy boots are a nice touch."

"I'm an Oriceran from Texas. Yumfuck wanted me to wear the hat too but I vetoed that idea."

"It could have worked." She wound a lock of his long blonde hair around her finger. "This has been a perfect day so far."

"So far." Correk scanned the street. "No one has thrown a fireball at our heads and no magical has suddenly needed rescuing from their own misdeeds."

"What do we tell them if you suddenly have to leave?"

"Turner said to tell anyone who asks that I work for the

No Such Agency. Locals would get it and just nod their heads."

"The NSA. Not a bad idea. You're not allowed to talk about your job and they're not supposed to ask." She wove her fingers between his, holding his hand. "Let's hope everyone can take a break from mayhem tonight."

The neighbor's door opened and Angel came out, talking in a steady stream to the tall man with close-cropped hair that was behind her, locking the door. He was giving her the occasional head nod.

"You're here!" Angel interrupted her flow of words to wave at Leira and Correk, going right back to the reminders she was giving for the next day.

"You didn't mention all the talking," whispered Correk.

"I kind of like it. You'll see." Leira squeezed his hand.

Angel was wearing a floral print dress that was in constant motion as she made her way quickly down the front steps, her hands moving in short gestures while she talked. "This is so exciting! I have been kerplumphed at the idea of friends who are next door neighbors. There is so much we could do. We could start a game night! Have you guys ever played Stupid Deaths? The best."

"You're right, it's oddly comforting. Like a wave of optimism," whispered Correk. Leira's smile grew as she listened to Angel with her husband waiting patiently by her side.

"We have seven-thirty reservations. Everybody okay with walking? Nice boots," said Angel, not waiting for a reply.

"I'm Matt, Angel's husband." He had an easy going smile, reaching out his hand to Correk to shake.

Angel laughed, covering her mouth with her carefully manicured hand. "I always forget that part. I mean, it already feels like we're friends. This is my husband, Matt. And that's Leira and you must be her boyfriend, Correk. They live right there."

Matt's smile grew as he shook Leira's hand. "How about we head down N Street and we can turn on twenty-third. It's a nice night for walking."

Leira's hand tingled for a moment against Matt's skin but it passed quickly. She took a longer look at him, still smiling. *Not a magical. Weird. Let it go, Berens. They're nice people.*

"It's a clear night but with all the lights it's hard to see the stars," said Angel.

Leira smiled, squeezing Correk's hand. They had their own planetarium to retreat to whenever they wanted.

"The best place in town is probably Rock Creek Park, right Matt?" asked Angel, as they started to walk toward the restaurant. Her husband nodded, putting his arm around his wife's shoulders. "No matter where you look, up or down, there's something beautiful. I love the walking trails in there. Matt loves to go running through there. You're a runner too, right, Leira?" Angel lifted her hair off the back of her neck. "Can you believe how warm it is tonight? That happens sometimes the closer we get to spring. Bam! You get this perfect evening for a stroll and then you're back to the heavy coat tomorrow."

Leira looked around at the different buildings as they walked, letting the words wash over her, grateful she didn't have to answer a lot of questions. *No Estelle to stop the inquiries. I will have to learn how to do it for myself.*

"Leira, have you been to the Air and Space museum yet?"

Leira opened her mouth to answer but Angel was already launching into a rundown of the best exhibits. Leira closed her mouth with a smile, feeling the last of her tension melting away. *A perfect day, still.*

They walked together down the wide boulevard to get to the restaurant, occasionally answering Angel's short questions.

Mostly Correk and Leira listened to the description of their new hometown through her eyes. Leira felt herself relax in a way she hadn't done in years. *Just for tonight. Give me this one night.*

They were shown to a table by a wall covered in faded blue shiplap near a clear plexiglass wall that held up wine bottles resting on clear pegs.

"It's nice, right?" Angel slid into her chair, her gold hoop earrings swinging and catching the soft overhead light.

"All the ingredients here are sourced locally," said Matt. "You two are from Texas, right? That's a big change. East Coast in a company town where politics is the company."

"I kind of like it," said Leira, peering at the menu. "Fewer trucks and boots but people are a lot alike."

"I take it you don't have to deal with lobbyists, then," said Matt, smiling.

The waiter came over to the table, dressed in a white shirt and black tie, a white apron tied at the waist. "Would you all care to start with wine?"

"What about a Chardonnay?" asked Angel, nodding at everyone. "We can get a bottle for the table. Does that work?"

"We have a crisp Chardonnay from Upper Shirley vineyard."

The waiter quickly returned with the bottle, filling glasses after it passed muster with Angel. "None for me," said Matt, placing his hand above his glass. "Sparkling water would be great."

"A little wine and I slow down a little," said Angel. "Like my motor was greased or something."

"That's why I keep some handy in the house," said Matt, laughing, as Angel swatted at him.

"Do you guys have kids?" asked Angel, despite the frown from Matt. "What? I thought I heard a child laughing in your house the other day."

"Must have been the TV," said Correk, taking a long sip from his wine and swallowing.

"What do you do for a living, Matt?" Leira shrugged at Correk, trying to change the subject.

"I'm an ER doc at GW University Hospital. It keeps me pretty busy. I spend an entire shift giving orders as fast as I can, moving as fast as I can."

"It's why he lets me talk so much," said Angel with a wink. "We're a pot and a lid. A perfect match."

"As soon as I walk out the doors all I want to do is slow down, notice everything, listen to anything but the sound of my own voice."

"I do their books, I'm in accounts receivable. That's where we met, in the cafeteria." Angel picked up her menu at the sight of the waiter returning to their table. "Could we have a few more minutes?"

He gave a quick nod and quickly retreated.

Angel leaned over the table. "The halibut is my favorite here."

"And the gouda and grits are my cheat for the week any time I can get it," said Matt. "What do you do Correk?"

Leira saw Correk freeze for a moment and relax again, sliding into the cover story. "I work for the No Say Agency." He pressed his lips together, not adding another word. The awkward silence hung there for a moment and for once, Leira filled it.

"I was a homicide detective back in Austin. I'm still figuring out what's next for me."

Leira reached for a roll, the same time as Matt, her knuckles brushing against the top of his hand. A spark traveled up her fingers and settled in her elbow. *There it is again.*

She smiled and waited for him to take a roll first, unable to see any hesitation. She smiled at Correk and looked at her menu, the question growing in her mind. *What kind of magical leaves no trail?*

"I am so full." Leira sat back, her hand on her belly, licking her lips. "This has been a very good day."

"It has, hasn't it?" asked Angel, clapping her hands together. "We should do this again."

"How about our house?" asked Correk, finishing the last of the wine in his glass.

Leira did her best to hide her surprise, mentally trying to count how much wine Correk had drunk. "Yeah, that would be great. We can... well, we can order out really well."

"That would do," laughed Matt. "Oh, hey, great timing. That's my pants buzzing." He reached into his pocket and pulled out his phone. "Shit, they're getting hammered." He stood up and Correk rose, putting his napkin on the table.

"No, you guys stay," said Angel. "You two look like you could use a little time alone," she said, smiling. "We'll grab an Uber and Matt can drop me off."

Matt got out his wallet but Correk was faster, handing a credit card to the waiter. "This one's on us. You were nice enough to tell us all about DC."

"It makes it feel more like home. Thank you," said Leira.

"If you two aren't the cutest." Angel leaned over to hug Leira in the same tight embrace as before. She scooped her purse off the table, smoothing out her dress. "Do you do yoga? That could be next on our list."

"We've got to go, hon," said Matt, nodding his head toward the door.

Angel and Matt were gone in a flurry of words and waving goodbye as Correk sat back down. "There's a list?" asked Correk, with an amused smile.

"It would probably take an Angel with a list to get me to do normal shit. She's like an Estelle on happy pills and without the cloud of smoke."

"You sound like you're looking forward to it. What have you done with my Leira?"

"Okay, fuck off. I'm still in here."

"That's better. You were giving me the willies."

"Did you notice anything weird about Matt? When I shook his hand there was a zing of energy that went straight up my arm."

"No, I didn't notice anything. Maybe he has that spark of humanity, like you."

Leira stood up, stretching her back. "Can that happen? I never thought of that."

"It's still a little early. You want to get dessert on the way home?"

"I would rather do something that's a little more custom for just you and me," said Leira.

"The fun under an ocean wasn't enough for you today?"

"Down big man. I was talking about the other worldly, spooky kind." They walked toward the door holding hands. "I think I found another thin place in the world."

The smile slipped from Correk's face. "You want to rescue Ossonia."

"As soon as possible. It's the end of a perfect day. Finding this could make it even better. It's hope that what happened in Paris could have a slightly different ending."

"Then let's do it. I'm your ride or die."

"I'm not positive you're using that right, but I appreciate the sentiment."

Wolfstan sat with his back to his desk, looking out the large windows at the manicured grounds to the Fleeker entrance far below. "Soon, Harkin will be back where he belongs in Trevilsom Prison and I will earn a place in the royal court. Irony abounds." He chuckled, turning his chair around and pulling in enough energy to make his eyes glow, sending a sprinkling of magic into the lock of the thin drawer on the right.

Click, click, tink.

He slid open the drawer, the sides of his mouth curling into a smile that froze in place. At first, he stared at the empty space, unable to believe someone had made it all the way into his office and into this drawer. He slammed his fist onto the desk. "The second damn infiltration!" He stood up, pacing behind his desk, shoving his chair out of the way. His assistant came running into the room, but he shooed the nervous young man away.

"Don't let me be disturbed." He waited till the door was closed and then searched the room for the telltale signs of a magical. "A clever magical," he sneered. He crouched down and ran his fingers over the few remaining marbles of Lily's magic, dabbing at it and pressing it to his tongue. "A witch." He spit on the carpet, wiping his tongue on a handkerchief from his back pocket. "I'll find you soon enough. No one is getting in my way. Not when I'm finally this close to everything."

CHAPTER SIXTEEN

L eira and Correk stood in front of the old house at 1799 New York Avenue. "This is it," said Leira. "Now we just have to break inside and go upstairs."

"You're a lot of fun on a date. How can you be sure no one's home?"

"The place has an inch of dust on everything and nothing sitting on any counters. No one's living here right now."

Correk waited for a jogger to pass behind them and get far enough away. "You think the ghosts drove them off?"

"Good question." Leira started to walk toward the house but Correk grabbed her hand.

"Every time you get anywhere near the world in between, the dark mist comes out to play. We need to proceed with extreme caution."

"Nothing appeared the last time I was here. Not a whiff, not a hum, nothing." She bit her bottom lip, raising her eyebrows. *Can't shake the feeling someone was following me. Probably not true.*

"That only makes me wonder when something hairy or slimy will try and crash the party." Correk watched the second story windows but there was no movement, no shadowy figures.

"We will both be on guard in there. This is only a fact finding trip. There's a lot to figure out before we try a rescue. We have to figure out how to find Ossonia first, then see if we can even pierce the veil. It's not like it's gotten any easier despite the creatures that have crawled out of there."

"I don't want to give Perrom any false hope."

"Then we don't tell him till we have something real that has some kind of chance of working." Leira smiled and nodded at a woman walking her schnauzer. "Let's get inside before someone starts to wonder why we're staring up at an empty house." Leira took off at a run in her sandals and dress, easily making it to the steps. "Race you to the front door."

Correk smiled but walked up more slowly, scanning the ground for trails of other magicals. A thrum of energy passed along the back of his neck, making him uneasy but no trails. "Nothing," he muttered, catching up with Leira. "Make it quick," he said. "You can do the honors."

Leira gave a crooked smile and her eyes glowed as she touched the handle, the lock turning with a click. The door popped open and the pair slid inside, Correk shutting the door behind them. "We make a great team."

"At breaking in places? Kind of not our thing."

Leira snorted and started up the stairs. "Can you feel the temperature change? It gets colder the higher you go up the stairs." She took the last few stairs at a run, jogging toward the bedroom where she had seen the woman on the other side.

"Only in our family would the chance of running into the dead make you run faster toward them." Correk still kept his slower pace, using the skills Turner Underwood had taught him, checking the area. "Still nothing." He gave a slight shake of his head but stopped short. The rumble of energy passed along the back of his neck again. His breathing slowed down, and he listened for the slightest sound. *Nothing.*

Leira poked her head out of the room. "Are you coming? What are you doing out here?" She saw the look of concern on his face and came all the way out into the hall-way, looking over the banister for any sign of trouble. "I don't sense anything."

"Something's off. I've felt a power surge twice."

"The tables have turned. You're now the cool kid with the really weird powers," said Leira, her eyes glowing as she sent out a stream of energy. "Nope, I've got nothing. How are you doing that?"

"Turner Underwood. When I started learning to be the Fixer, he taught me how to feel the streams of magic all the time on a low level. Then when somebody's in trouble..."

"You feel it. You're like a kind of telegraph machine."

"Or Twitter if you want to join me in this century." Correk walked by Leira into the bedroom, putting his hand against the wall. A shock went up his arm, setting off tiny sparks.

"Oooh, I saw that one," said Leira, following him back into the room and putting her hand on the wall. "Wow, still nothing. I'm not sure I like being left out of the party."

"Is that what we're calling mayhem now?" He lifted his chin. "You party plenty without me."

"Okay, I can share. You ready to do this thing?" Leira rubbed her hands together in the darkened room. The only light was coming from the bare windows overlooking the street.

"There's nothing here. I don't sense anything."

"Yeah, but I have an idea." Leira stood in the center of the room. "This is where the woman was pushing out from the world in between, and we both know that place has it bad for me."

"I'm vetoing this idea."

But it was too late. Leira was letting the energy flow through her and the symbols along her arms were flipping over. Slow at first but picking up speed.

Correk read the symbols and stepped closer to Leira, his muscles tense. "Your magic can't read the future this time. It must be running up against the endless time in the world in between."

Leira opened her mouth to say something but instead sucked in, air filling her lungs, the pressure mounting against her chest. She rocked back on her heels doing her best to clear her mind and let the magic lead. *Don't panic, hold steady.*

Unsure what to do, Correk placed his hand on Leira's shoulder but there was no magic to siphon off.

Her head felt lighter and the room was growing fuzzy as she dropped to her knees. The air in the room was still pushing into her mouth, suffocating her.

Leira squeezed her eyes shut and called out to the one

person who might be able to help. Another Jasper Elf. *Dad, I need you.*

There were pinpoints of light flashing in her brain as she struggled to stay conscious and Correk began uttering ancient spells, to no avail.

A weak spot in the room the size of a quarter began to shimmer, bulging out toward Leira.

Leira opened her eyes, staring at Correk, her lips turning blue as a stream of glittering silver energy wrapped around them both, climbing up Leira's body and circling her head, eventually pushing back at the shimmering circle.

A blue flame spread across the circle, pulling it wider. Faces could be seen squeezing together behind it. The pressure eased on Leira's chest and the air rushed out of her lungs, giving her the chance to take in small sips of air. Correk crouched between her and the opening, staring at the tormented and trapped beings.

He reached his hand out, but the heat of the flame made him pull back.

"Dad... Dad... Dad..." Leira spit out, unable to get enough oxygen to say much more.

"Is that your father's energy?" Correk watched with wonder as Jackson's light surrounded the growing opening, thinning it out till the faces became more visible. "There is a way," he said, awed.

The Jasper Elf's energy wound a tighter and tighter circle, closing down the opening until it was just a pinhole, disappearing altogether. The swirl of shimmering light circled back around Leira, finally pulling back out of the room.

Leira fell back, lying flat on the floor, still taking in longer and longer breaths, blowing out all the air before trying again. "That was new," she said, hoarsely. "Just when I think I know what the hallway from hell can throw at me, it comes up with a new twist."

"I think I see a way to get Ossonia out, if we can find her," said Correk excitedly.

Leira turned her head to get a better look at him, finally breathing easier. "You and I are having very different experiences." She pushed herself up to a sitting position, letting Correk help her to her feet. "Next time we come here, I'm wearing pants."

"You and your father together. Two Jasper Elves. I think you could punch a hole through and make a door."

Leira leaned against Correk's muscled chest. "Dad. He showed up pretty fast. Thank goodness."

Correk wrapped his arms around Leira, pressing her closer. "I spent so many years thinking family was unnecessary. I think I may have been wrong. Both our fathers may prove to be the answer to a few different questions."

Leira smiled, patting his chest. "Now you're talking. See, still a perfect evening. Okay, okay, there was that five minutes but out of twenty-four hours, not bad odds."

"Really good ones if you're talking about us," said Correk, kissing the top of her head. "Ossonia, we are coming for you."

CHAPTER SEVENTEEN

Toby Wheeler stood in the darkness of the city street, tapping his wand against his shaking leg. "Why didn't I quit when I had the chance?"

"Because you never learned how to do anything else and you would have starved." Isabel was dressed in a long dark trench coat, cinched at the waist.

"What's with the Jane Bond look?"

"Deflects water," she said, pulling out her wand. "I figure it'll do the same with canine blood."

Toby let out a frustrated sigh, walking a circle around Isabel. "How long are we supposed to wait here? What makes anyone think we'll even spot a shifter?"

"Can you stop your whining? You make it hard to hear anything else. It's bad enough I got stuck with you just because I was in close proximity"

"Hey, I know what I'm doing. I'm an asset."

"We'll see. But I'm betting if it goes south, I can run faster than you, and that's all I'll need."

"Thanks, Cousin."

"Shhhh, wait." Isabel lifted her chin, listening, her wand held out in front of her. "Something is coming toward us. Are you crying?"

"No, the wind blew in my face."

"You'd better get ready. It's looking like the informant was right. This is a regular route for a few of our furry friends."

Toby peered through the starless night trying to hold his wand steady. "Hey, that's just a man," he whispered.

"Just wait."

The tall figure was silhouetted against the trees as he walked down Luzon Avenue and turned onto Nebraska where Isabel and Toby were waiting.

A sliver of moon hung in the sky, barely lighting anything below. Toby watched pensively as the man took off for a jog toward the park.

"Come on, it's a jogger."

"At three a.m. in Rock Creek Park? You're out here this time of night, you're looking for trouble or you got nowhere else to go." Isabel gripped her wand and took off in the direction of the man.

The man passed briefly under a streetlight, illuminating dark thick hair cut short around his ears, wearing a hoodie and jeans.

"Nobody told me to wear running shoes," hissed Toby, doing his best to keep up with Isabel. They crossed over Sixteenth Street and went into the darkened park running and stopping for over a mile, listening for the sound of a twig breaking or branches being pushed aside.

"I think we lost him," said Toby, breathing hard next to Isabel.

Isabel pinched the soft underside of Toby's arm and scowled at him, baring her teeth. "Be quiet!"

Toby's mouth formed a large 'O', but he said nothing and looked in the direction Isabel was pointing with her wand.

A naked man was bent forward, his arms stretched out wide as the bones twisted and reformed, the sound of bones cracking reaching the young witch and wizard. Toby pressed his hand to his stomach and swallowed hard.

Fur sprouted first along the ridge of his back, working its way out to his extremities. His head bowed, the jaw growing longer as the man shifted, his front paws softly touching down on the ground.

Slowly, the shifter pushed up on his hind legs, snarling and growling until the pain of his change subsided. He stretched his back legs and took a deep breath, bowing his head down and moving his shoulders.

The animal crept out of the trees and stood for a moment in the center of the park, howling loudly, lifting his head toward the moon. The noise rose into the air to echo across the park.

"Yip, yip, yip!" The sounds of other shifters answered the call. The wolf howled again, stopping abruptly and sniffing the air.

The large, furry head swung in the direction of the young magicals, the lips pulled back to reveal large fangs as the shifter growled. Toby bit his bottom lip, tasting blood and held out his wand. He held his breath, his eyes wide doing his best not to think about the last time he had been faced with shifters.

"I can do this," he muttered.

"Of course you can. I would have knocked you out and left you for bait by now if I didn't think so." Isabel made small circles with her wand and snapped it forward, winding out a light of gold studded with thorns. The magical lasso wrapped around the back leg of the shifter, digging in and drawing blood. The wolf whipped his head around, biting at the light with his teeth, easily cutting through it and turning it to ashes.

"Wait, that's not supposed to be possible," said Isabel, the color draining from her face, her eyes wide.

"What the fuck?" Toby looked down at his hard-soled shoes and scanned the nearby trees, calculating which one he could climb fast enough to get out of the way.

The yipping grew louder as the other shifters closed in on the location. The wolf in front of them lifted his snout and howled out a plaintive cry that ended in a loud, high-pitched note. The sound of the other shifters increased, breaking into a chorus of yips and howls that seemed to grow closer, faster.

"What the fuck have we done?" yelled Toby. "You know he just told the entire pack what you did."

"What we did." Isadora stood firm with her wand but seemed to hesitate. "Oh, fuck it." She took off at a run in the opposite direction, her wand still in her hand, not looking back over her shoulder.

Toby watched her go, his mind reeling with what to do next. He finally ran in a zigzag pattern up the middle of the park in a blind panic. "Don't look at what's chasing you.

Don't look at what's chasing you." He kept repeating the mantra, spittle dropping on his shirt.

He came to the creek that ran through the park and dashed into it, wading across with no particular destination in mind. He slid on a rock, landing on his ass, the water splashing up around his face and scrambled to his knees, crawling the rest of the way out of the creek. His hands were bruised, and his face was scratched from running through the dense trees, but it didn't matter. He kept running until he realized the sound had grown more distant.

He stopped for a moment, his heart pounding so loudly he heard a buzzing in his ears, trying to focus on where the yipping was coming from now.

"Southeast corner." A look of horror came over his face and he looked in that direction and back over his shoulder. "Isabel." He held out his shaking wand, steadying it with his other hand and tapped the air three times. "Find me her heart, dark as this night."

The sound of Isabel's heart echoed from the tip of his wand, slowing fading until it finally stopped. Toby leaned over, his hand pressing against the bark of a tree and threw up the contents of his dinner, tears filling his eyes. He took his wand and broke it over his knee, a dark thread of magic pouring out of it.

He pulled out his phone, blinking back tears and pulled up his mother's number. *I'm coming home*, he texted. *I've had enough. I'm sorry.*

He started to walk in his wet shoes for the far side of the park when a *bing* sounded from his phone and he held it up to his face. *There is always a place for you here. We'll figure it out together like a family. Hurry home.*

Toby wiped his face on a dry part of his sleeve and swallowed hard, putting his phone away and trudging out of the park.

CHAPTER EIGHTEEN

Louie sidestepped a pair of hedgehogs burrowing under the raised garden behind Ghouls Tavern deep in the Dark Forest. "That is not gonna go over well with Markette, guys. You've been warned."

The door to the tavern suddenly flew open and a Dwarf tumbled out, end over end, landing flat on his back. "Nice to see you again Jolly. I see your day is going well."

"You too, Louie," groaned Jolly, shutting his eyes and making no attempt to get out of the dirt. A third hedgehog scurried around him, heading for the same hole toward the side of the bar.

Louie went into the darkened bar, walking across the uneven floor to the long oak bar, taking a seat on a stool. He shifted the sword strapped to his back and swiveled on the seat to get a better view of the rest of the tavern.

"Hey, Louie," said the bartender. Her hair was pulled back in a loose ponytail and a smear of eyeliner from last night was still under her eyes. "Your usual?"

"Sure, hit me, Markette," Louie replied, looking around the dim bar. "Where's Hairy and his brother, Fang?" Louie took a slow look around the bar, peering into the darkened corners for his connection. *Not here yet.*

Markette snorted, putting a glass of whiskey down in front of Louie. "Kilomeas don't take well to body shaming, Louie, especially those two brothers. Haven't they kicked your ass enough for one lifetime?"

"It's become our thing. We have a bromance going on, even if they don't know it." He took a sip, the warmth spreading down his throat. "I've gotten in a few good licks myself," he said with a wink.

Markette smiled, shaking her head at him. "I must have been off those days." Markette reached under the bar and pulled out an envelope, slapping it on the bar. "This came for you while you were gone." Markette gave him a long look. "You sure you know what you're doing?"

Louie raised his eyebrows in surprise. "I always know enough for the next five minutes, give or take a minute."

Markette rolled her eyes and went back to wiping glasses. "One of these days, Louie, that charm won't be enough to get you out of whatever death defying hole you dug for yourself."

"Make sure you serve everyone the good whiskey at my wake. I don't want anyone saying I was a cheap bastard." He opened the envelope and read the short message. *Meet me out back behind the first stand of poplars.* The words quickly changed into worms, wriggling on the page.

"Take those outside," growled Markette, sampling some of the gin.

"I'll go feed the birds. Don't take my drink," he said,

pulling out a handful of pintas and tossing them on the bar. "I'll be back."

"Yes, but will it be today?" called Markette, as Louie pushed through the door and went outside, stepping over Jolly, snoring in the dirt.

He came around the back of the thatch-covered building and walked through the thick undergrowth, making his way to the stand of trees. He stepped past the first line of poplars and a beefy hand reached out to grab him, pulling him further inside. He neatly slid his wand out of a pocket, the start of a spell on his lips.

"Point that thing somewhere else," the Kilomea growled.

"What's with all the drama, Bruce? There's a perfectly good bar right over there with chairs and alcohol. Why are we playing in the woods?"

"I have news on Sirius," he whispered. "Your boy is playing a very dangerous game. There's talk around the Dark Market that there's a new player who's doing the impossible."

Louie waited, shaking his head. "You'll need to be more specific about what impossible means. We need a dramatic pause? Come on, give me the goods."

"You're ruining this for me."

"Sorry, let me try again. Oh my God! What is it?"

"Okay, now you're just fucking with me."

"Most magicals think Kilomeas are big lugs who like to steal shit and kill things."

"And now you're hurting my feelings."

Louie patted him on his bulky arm. "But I know better. You do like to steal shit and kill things, though."

"Truth. Most of my cousins would like to hunt you

down." The Kilomea grew somber, putting his hands on Louie's shoulders, the weight pressing down on the wizard. "Enough with the bullshit. If you're messing around with Sirius, you've pulled yourself into something beyond both of us this time. The new player is making a name for himself in both worlds. He's gaining power in the royal court and there's talk he has power on Earth, too."

"Ah, the impossible," muttered Louie. "Fuck, this is bad."

"Sirius has signed up to help him, but I'm not sure it was altogether voluntary, or that there's any kind of out clause that doesn't involve dismemberment."

"Ouch. That would sting. Where can I find Sirius?"

"You're still gonna hunt him down. I have to give you respect. When they find pieces of you can I have the sword?" Bruce reached out to touch it, but a spark flew out and stung his hand.

"It kind of has to choose you, big guy. Sirius?"

"He's in the other world, in Washington, DC. He's on tap to take down Leira Berens or die trying. In exchange he gets protection and the chance to control a section of their world."

"Who is powerful enough to first convince Sirius that's even doable and then attempt to pull it off? Most important, where can I find Sirius?"

"He goes by Wolfstan Humphrey. Bad Light Elf did a stretch in Trevilsom and came out with his mind intact. That is some serious magic."

"Narrow it down for me a little more. Where exactly can I find Sirius. DC is a big city."

"You have the artifact I wanted?"

"I have it. First an address."

The Kilomea shook his head. "That won't work. Sirius moves around every few days. He's gotten paranoid and with good reason. I'm not sure he has the complete backing of the families anymore."

"Then our deal is off."

"Now hold on. I have something even better. Sirius checks in every day with Wolfstan. He uses the old trapping spell."

"Right, it's impenetrable and perfect for sending messages you don't want anyone else to see." Louie scowled, getting that itchy feeling to get moving. That feeling had saved him more than once.

"That's usually true. But I have a gift for you." Bruce reached into the pocket of his cloak. "It can't do much for me. I'm not willing to tangle with Sirius or Wolfstan Humphrey." He held out a purple geode. "Every relic starts as something ordinary till a magical infuses it with magic. This one used to belong to Sirius and still has his signature."

Louie's eyes widened with delight. "You are a genius. Worth some of your weight in gold." He took the artifact from Bruce, turning it over in his hands. "It'll act as a GPS for Sirius."

"Once it gets within a hundred miles of him. And if you get lucky with the timing of the trapping spell..."

Louie spun in a circle. "We might be able to track Wolfstan too."

Bruce grinned, his large canine teeth showing. "That should work for your purposes."

"Like a charm." Louie reached into his satchel, pulling out a drawstring pouch and securing the geode. He pushed it toward the bottom and pulled out a larger drawstring bag, loosening the top and sliding out a wooden music box. "Per our deal. You've earned it. A music box that can help anyone fall in love with you." Louie shook his head. "You are a giant, hairy marshmallow, Bruce."

Bruce grinned, his large molars protruding, taking the box from Louie.

"Don't open it here!" Louie put a hand on the top. "I like you, Bruce, but let's not take it any further. I don't need to be under your spell. You sure you know what you're doing?"

"I'm sure. I have my eye on a Kilomea from the mountains. She has three suitors, all with more money than I've got. I can't lose her."

Louie smiled, patting him on the back, raising a small cloud of dust. "Good luck to you. I hope it's everything you want."

Bruce looked at Louie solemnly. "You too, Louie. Be careful. You've never gone up against forces like this. I'd kind of miss you."

"Bruce, that is the nicest thing a Kilomea has ever said to me. You're one of a kind. I hate to leave you here, but time is not on my side on this one."

Bruce patted Louie on the shoulder, jarring him a little. "No, it is not. Get out of here, and before anyone sees us together. I don't want that geode being traced back to me. Be safe, Louie."

"That's not in my cards, Bruce." Louie ducked out from

the trees and made his way through the brush till he could find a clearing and create a portal. He circled his wand, opening up a space into his apartment and stepping through, reaching for his phone he had left on the counter. "Three a.m. I'm texting her anyway."

CHAPTER NINETEEN

L eira stood at the kitchen window sipping a glass of water looking out at the alley. She had woken up in the middle of the night, her chest still aching from the run in with the world in between and had crept quietly downstairs.

Bang!

A trash can hit a wall and rolled on its side, clattering against cobblestones. Leira put down the glass and quietly opened the back door, stepping outside, staying back in the shadows.

She saw the outline of a large dog limping down the alley and narrowed her gaze, watching the creature move. "Shifter," she whispered, her body growing tense as she gripped the railing.

The shifter's back leg was wounded, and he was winded, gingerly stepping across the stones till he got to the neighbor's back door.

Angel Moss opened her back door, the light from her kitchen shining out on the shifter.

"Oh my God," she exclaimed, running down the steps, petting the large head of the shifter and running back inside, only to reappear with a bath towel to hold against the leg.

Leira's face changed to surprise as she watched the shifter nudge Angel away from him and he braced his three good legs. His bones twisted with a loud crunch, shifting back into human form. The head lifted back into place and the jaw shortened as the hair sunk into the skin until standing under the light was the naked form of Matt Moss. There was a gaping wound along his left calf and blood was oozing out of it.

That explains the buzz I kept getting from him. Leira pressed back against the wall of her house.

"You lost your best track suit. No matter," said a nervous Angel, draping her husband's arm over her shoulder. "Good thing you showed me how to do stitches. What the hell happened out there?"

"We were ambushed. One of them got away."

Angel looked around to see if anyone was out, but Leira was tucked too far into the corner for Angel to see. She helped her husband up the steps, talking to him the whole way, reassuring him that everything would be alright.

Leira went back into the kitchen, quietly closing the door just as Correk came into the room, his hand on the light.

"Don't turn that on," said Leira. "Keep it dark."

"What's happened?" Correk came and stood next to her, looking out the window.

"This is a very small world. I just saw our neighbor,

Matt shift from a wolf back into human form and he was injured."

"Did they see you?"

"No, and for now I'm going to keep their secret. But how did he get injured? He said something about a trap. I know what you're thinking but why would the Dark Families bother with a local pack?"

"Better question is how did anyone find them?"

"A traitor. That's a new wrinkle. Why does it seem like there are traitors everywhere?"

Leira's phone buzzed on the kitchen counter. She picked it up and looked at the text from Louie.

I have some intel that can't wait. On my way over.

"It looks like everyone is up tonight," said Correk with a yawn.

"Go back to bed. I can keep Louie company. I wonder if Matt is a part of Lucius' pack."

"Something for when the sun is up."

"What's up?" Leira sat across her kitchen table from Louie, watching him inhale a leftover piece of pot roast.

"You eat like Yumfuck."

"I live on Chinese food, so give me a fucking break." Louie replied, wiping his mouth.

"Whatever you found out has you keyed up. I take it, it was useful."

Louie nodded his head, folding another piece with his hand and stuffing it in his mouth. He held up a finger, chewing as fast as he could and swallowed, sitting back in the chair with an exhausted sigh.

"You know, I could have probably waited till morning for this information."

"No, information goes stale pretty fast. Sticking to that rule is what made me into a primo scavenger." He got up and looked in the refrigerator grabbing a jar of green olives off the door.

"Whenever you're ready..." Leira rested her chin in her hand.

Louie opened the jar with a pop, pulling out a few and sliding them into his mouth. "There's a bounty on your head."

"Not new information and shut the fridge."

"Yeah, well, the Dark Families have company. Wolfstan Humphrey wants you dead and he's using Sirius to do it."

"We already know all of this."

"Sirius is in town, planning something.'"

Leira sat up straighter. "I suspected as much. It's not a secret where I'm living."

"Yeah, your wards on this house are impressive. But I'm not sure they're going to be enough. They're taking their time planning this one. And, Wolfstan has it for you bad. If he recruited Sirius..."

"Then there might be others. The thought has occurred to me."

Louie wiped his hands on a dish towel. "Here's where you see how valuable I am to the team." He pulled out the drawstring bag and opened it, easing out the geode. "It's an artifact with Sirius' magic contained in it." Louie bobbed his head in excitement, rolling his eyes when Leira didn't react.

"I'm sensing this is a really good thing."

"Sometimes I forget how new you are to the magic of it all." He sat back down at the table and held the geode out for her, waving his other hand around enthusiastically. "In our world, this is as good as a GPS if we can get within a hundred miles of Sirius. Yeah? Now you get it."

Leira picked up the geode and felt the buzz of magic passing through it.

"But wait, there's more. A possible bonus. If we use something called the trapping spell at the same moment as Sirius or Wolfstan does and Sirius is within range of this geode, it will also locate Wolfstan."

"Will they know someone has tracked them?"

Louie shook his head. "No fucking way."

"You are brilliant," said Leira, hugging Louie around his neck. "You know, this is the second time you've brought me an artifact that just might save my life."

"Just doing my job, ma'am."

"Now show me how to find Sirius and the trapping spell."

Leira sat in the darkened kitchen alone holding the geode. "No time like the present." She centered herself, breathing in deeply and letting it out, holding the geode in her hand. Energy flowed in through her feet and up through her body, lighting up the symbols along her arms. She set an intention letting her stream of magic seek out the energy contained in the stone. "Find the source," she sang into the geode, the two threads of magic intertwining and flowing together.

The energy flowed back and forth, looking for its source, but there was no sign of Sirius.

"Try again," Leira whispered fervently in the darkness. "He's here somewhere."

Again, the magic sped over the ground, searching everywhere but retreated, coming back with nothing.

Leira felt her heart sink, wondering if the geode was just a pretty rock.

Her phone buzzed on the table and she looked up at the clock. Five a.m., not even dawn. "What is with this night? Hello Hagan, what's up? It's even earlier where you are."

"You had better get here. There's something happening on the outskirts of the sanctuary. The Gardener's alarms picked it up and he sent out some birds or drones, I don't know. There's a small army building up out there and there's a familiar silver-haired wizard at the front of the pack."

A chill settled in Leira's bones. The geode may not have worked, but she knew where Sirius was in that moment.

"You'd better hurry. Harkin keeps talking about going out there with the Gardener, but I don't think they're enough to fight off that pack. I've called Lois and she had a few choice words to say about her brother. I think she wants to take him out herself. She's letting Lacey Trader know, but it looks bad."

"What about Rose?"

Hagan's voice cracked, the first time Leira had ever heard that and it broke her heart.

"If something happens to her because I took her to this place..."

"We won't let that happen. Put her somewhere safe. We are all on our way. Sirius is trying to pick a fight. Let's give him one and cut off Wolfstan, at least from the Dark Families."

"Hurry kid."

"I'm almost there. I just need to grab Correk and Yumfuck."

CHAPTER TWENTY

Leira stepped through the portal two hundred feet to the right of the assembled witches and wizards from the Dark Families, flanking them. Correk slipped through next with the troll on his shoulder, pulling the portal closed and stepping on any sparks. They were hidden by a thin stand of trees with a clear view of the congregation gathered at the base of the hill that lead up to the sanctuary. "There looks to be about a hundred of them and it's the old guard. I don't see many young witches or wizards with them," said Correk, crouching behind the tree. His longbow was strapped to his back and a sword tied at his waist.

"Where did he find enough of the older dark forces to follow him?"

"Sirius lead the families for a very long time. There were bound to be those still loyal to him. It doesn't matter what he's done. They still believe him when he says he will help them keep their rightful place."

"Lois got in touch with Lacey Trader. The Silver

Griffins are coming in force. But Sirius had to know this would be our response, and there are very powerful wards around this place. What makes him look so confident?"

"Arrogance to begin with, but there's an even bigger question. How did they find this place? Wolfstan Humphrey has to be helping them."

"We may not be taking him seriously enough if he can do this." Leira ducked down as the crowd looked up at a crack of thunder. Clouds gathered overhead, darkening the sky. "Lois said to wait for the signal and we would know it when we saw it." Yumfuck jumped from Correk's shoulder and came to stand by Leira, resting a paw on her shoe. "This waiting is not easy," she said.

The air shimmered next to them and a portal began to open. Correk pulled out an arrow but Leira stopped him. "By the way, I reached out to one more person before we left."

A portal opened just wide enough for Jackson to step through. Mara and Eireka were hard on his heels, followed by Louie.

"You brought Mom and Nana?" hissed Leira.

"I'm gonna assume you aren't worried about me because you know I'm a badass," said Louie.

"We would have skewered him from stem to stern if he had left us out and you were in danger," said Mara. "It took a bit of doing to get us all in the same room and figure out the coordinates, but baby girl when you need us, we will always come running. Where's Harkin?"

"He's inside the sanctuary, protecting it from that side," said Correk.

"Do we know if they can even breach the place?" asked Eireka, squeezing Leira's hand.

"We don't but we have to assume they have something."

"How did they find it?" asked Jackson, kissing Leira on the top of her head.

"I suspect Wolfstan has a way of tracking Harkin," said Leira, looking at Louie. "I have a hunch Wolfstan has something with Harkin's magic in his possession."

"That would be a fine piece of irony," said Louie.

"We can work on that problem after this one."

"Look," said Louie, "something's happening."

Sirius waved a new hickory wand, putting his hand up to shush the group. He stepped forward, lightning flashing across the sky and motioned for them to spread out into groups of three.

"Do we go yet?" asked Mara. Jackson moved up to the front, his eyes glowing and the symbols along his arms flipping over furiously. "Things are about to start," he said calmly. "Leira, as your dad, I want to ask you to stay toward the back. But I know there's no chance of that so I'm gonna ask you to take out as many as you can, as quickly as you can."

The air shimmered across the field to the left of the dark witches and wizards opening a mammoth portal.

"I have a feeling that's our signal," said Leira, standing up straight. She grabbed Correk by the arm. "If it's the last good thing we do."

"Today we fight with honor and to the end," he answered, kissing her as he held the back of her head.

"They are here," Sirius growled. "Leira, show yourself!"

Witches and wizards from the Silver Griffins poured

out of the opening, their wands drawn, running to create a semi-circle around the dark forces. Lacey Trader and Lois and Patsy were at the front, Lois shaking her head at her brother. "You never seem to learn," she shouted.

"I just have to be me," he shouted back. Sirius held up his hand, signaling his side to wait, their wands aimed at the approaching Silver Griffins.

"A lot of them have to be related to each other," said Mara. She looked around at everyone near her. "At least we can say all our family is fighting on the same side."

Leira turned to the others and nodded. "You ready?"

"Always," Mara replied, rubbing her hands together. "If those students of mine could see me now."

"I've *been* ready," Jackson said with a smile. "It's been a while since we've fought side by side, Mara. Like old times. Let's do this thing."

Prepare. The sword vibrated in Louie's hands. "Ready."

"For Ossonia," Correk growled through gritted teeth.

Yumfuck snarled, growing until he towered over them, stretching to his full height of eight feet tall.

Leira put her hands on Correk's shoulders and looked him in the eyes. She could feel the rush of revenge creeping into him.

"We have be let go of any anger," she warned, looking him in the eyes. "He knows she's your weak spot, and he'll use that to get you to make mistakes. You are the new Fixer and you know so much more than you did even last year. We will get Ossonia out and Sirius will pay for what happened in Paris. He'll pay for all of it. For Alan and the other agents. All of it."

Correk's expression softened, and he nodded, rubbing

his thumb across her cheek. Leira smiled and walked to the front taking her place next to Jackson, pulling energy up through her body. A ball of fire grew in her hands and Leira stepped out from behind the trees, her family by her side. Sirius spun around, immediately raising his wand, sneering at Leira. "At last!" he cried out, lowering his wand, the two sides abruptly running at each other.

Leira pitched the first volley, throwing the fireball in a curve that circled near Sirius, making him duck, hitting the wizard just behind him to his right and taking out some of his personal protection. Sirius scowled but he returned fire, whipping his wand across his chest and unleashing a curtain of fire, traveling rapidly at Eireka and Mara.

Leira's jaw clenched and the energy stormed through her.

"I've got this," yelled her grandmother, turning her hand in a clockwise motion, spinning the curtain of orange flames into a pillar and tipping it over onto a trio of witches. "That was satisfying. Oof!" She spun slightly to the left, a fireball punching her shoulder. Eireka moved to stand in front of her, returning fire.

"There you are!" Sirius exclaimed, walking slowly toward Leira, the fight going on all around him. "Here I thought you weren't going to answer my invitation."

"This has to end, Sirius. You've fallen so far down the ladder you've become someone's lame bitch," she said through gritted teeth, throwing a fireball straight at his chest.

The others stepped out beside him as Sirius dove to the side, the ball of energy slamming hard against the glamour the Gardener had put in place, shaking it at the foundation.

"He needs a Jasper Elf to break the wards," Leira yelled to her father. "Careful where you aim."

Sirius kept his eyes fixed on Leira as he got up from the ground, anger burning in his chest. "Kill them all!" he yelled, shooting sparks into the clouds as they broke open and rain began to fall.

Both sides took off running across the pasture, screaming loudly as they ran into battle.

Yumfuck's fur was already singed on one side as he pushed into the middle of the fighting, swiping his claws at a wizard aiming at Eireka, taking him out of the battle for good.

Patsy and Lois stood apart from each other aiming their wands to create an arc of energy over the heads of two wizards, threads of energy shooting off the arc, destabilizing their wands. "Now Patsy!" The two witches started turning the arc like a giant jump rope, catching different witches and wizards and knocking them over like bowling pins.

Leira fired round after round of fireball at Sirius, holding him back. But she was suddenly distracted by a figure running down the hill from the sanctuary. "Hagan! No!" Hagan was running faster than Leira had ever seen him move, passing easily through the wards, his gun drawn. Near the bottom he aimed at a wizard caught in battle with a witch from the Silver Griffins, catching the wizard in the shoulder. The magical grabbed his arm and screamed, dropping his wand. Hagan adjusted his pants and kept moving.

"What the fuck are you doing down here?" yelled Leira over the din.

"Protecting my home. I'm not waiting for the fight to come to me. When have you ever known me to make you fight alone? Don't look at me like that, kid. The Gardener and Harkin are protecting the sanctuary."

"How did you get Harkin to stay put?"

"I didn't, it was the Gardener. He spelled out that Harkin owed him, and he was going to help him protect the animals within the forest. I thought those two were going to fight each other for a second." Hagan shot off another round, barely missing a witch, running to help Patsy and Lois.

Correk found himself surrounded by two witches and two wizards, barely fighting them off. Sirius came from the other side, crouching low enough to wave his wand over the grass. Large patches of the grass began to tear and reshape itself, forming into short figures with a head and arms and legs. The first one reached Patsy, grabbing at her ankle as grass grew from its hands, twisting around her limb. Louie swung his sword, taking off the grassman's head, but it didn't stop it. The headless pile of grass and roots pulled at Patsy's leg, even as she wielded her wand in the opposite direction, spewing thorns at the encroaching witches.

Tilt the blade slightly to the right, swing at a thirty degree angle.

Louie didn't hesitate. He took the direction from the sword and swung again, cutting off the grassy fingers inches from Patsy's flesh. She wrenched her leg away just as Lois was finally able to get to her, sweat glistening on her forehead. "That was a close shave!" she yelled, helping her friend fend off attackers.

The other grass figure reached Correk with Sirius closing in on him, dodging the arrows and their magic. A wizard lunged for Correk as Sirius yelled, "Get the ring! Search for the ring!"

Correk shoved a boot square in the man's chest, cracking a rib and followed it with a kick to the head, knocking him unconscious. A grassman reached for him and he pulled out his sword, slicing off the arms as another approached. Louie joined him, turning his sword right and left, never missing, till they were all destroyed. Sirius retreated behind a wall of his followers, running behind the front line. He slid the sword back into its sheath, holding up the longbow again, aiming carefully.

Lacey let out an angry whoop in the distance, her velour top ripped at the shoulder and a bruise across her cheek. A witch closed in on her, too close to raise her wand and Lacey leaned back, settling for landing a punch squarely in the center of the witch's face.

Correk shot off an arrow, watching it turn in mid-flight, piercing a wizard who fell to the ground. He fired off another, narrowly missing a group of witches, the arrow whizzing past them. It got him close enough to Hagan to take out the sword. "Your gun isn't going to work for long, Hagan," he shouted, holding out the sword. "Do you think you can handle this?"

"I know enough. The Gardener has been giving me lessons." He slipped his gun into its holster.

Leira looked at him, her brow furrowed.

"What? I get bored easily." He shrugged. "I guess I'm not as cut out for a desk job as I thought. Correk, let me have it."

He held up the sword, admiring it. "This is a beauty. Has some real heft." A flash of light caught his eye.

He turned just before a fireball reached his head, ducking and slicing through it with the sword. The orb split in half and fell to the ground, sending out sparks in every direction that burned the grass, leaving black streaks.

The wizard tried again, throwing another fireball as Hagan held up the sword like a bat, smacking the flaming orb and sending it back, barely missing the wizard on its return flight. Hagan stomped over to him, grabbed him by the neck of his robe, and lifted him into the air, brandishing the sword and running on adrenaline.

"You messed with the wrong human," he bellowed, hitting the wizard over the head with the hilt of the sword. He threw the unconscious magical to the ground and stomped on his wand, breaking it in half. "I missed this."

Slice right, left, turn and jab. Louie's sword pushed him through every move, taking out one magical after another while he twisted and turned his wand with his other hand, sending out a spray of pea-sized fireballs in all directions.

Lois ducked, but one singed the top of her head. She pushed her glasses up her nose, glaring at Louie.

"Friendly fire. My apologies," he yelled, turning back and sending a ball of light swirling around the field, knocking several witches off their feet.

Lois patted the top of her head, going back into the fray and dodging a fireball only to be hit in the right shoulder by a stream of dark light. The magic spun her around and dropped her to the ground, smoke rising off her shirt. Patsy ran to her and went down on her knees, running her wand over the wound. "Earl is gonna have my head if I let anything happen to you. Not to mention you're my best friend and it took me years to get used to you."

"You have a weird way of paying a compliment, but I'll take it."

"It's the best I can do for now," said Patsy, helping Lois to her feet. "Can you still fight?"

"I've still got the one good wing. Let's go cause some trouble."

At the base of the hill, Leira stood back to back with Lacey Trader, fighting off a ring of wizards who had surrounded them. Leira set an intention, letting a stream of magic wrap around the wizards' legs, pulling tight as the bracelet jangled on her wrist.

"These assholes are tough," Leira growled, blocking a spell.

"They're desperate and that can sometimes give people hidden strength. It's too bad they couldn't think of a better way to use it. They think they're out here preserving something precious."

"Lead by Sirius. Duck!" They crouched down as a large pulse of energy blew over their heads, knocking down four wizards, cracking several ribs. "Thanks Mom!"

Eireka smiled, her hair falling around her shoulders. She ran to join Jackson and fight by his side.

"He makes them believe they have a vote." Lacey held out her wand, yelling, "Spinas et tribulos germinabit!" Nettles flew out of the end of her wand in rapid fire, piercing the skin of a witch and wizard.

"Nicely done," said Leira, her eyes glowing.

Lacey nodded her head. "Did I ever tell you that Sirius tried to join the Silver Griffins when he was young? It's true and we considered it, but he was a con artist even then. He couldn't tell the truth and we kicked him out."

"So, this is personal for him."

"Everything is personal for Sirius."

Louie came rushing by them, swinging the sword, pushing back the dark magicals.

Lacey spotted Sirius waving his wand at the wards, muttering spells feverishly, determined to break into the sanctuary.

"Oh, *hell* no." Lacey marched through the throng, throwing magicals out of her way with a flick of her wand, determined to get to Sirius.

"Fool," snarled Sirius. He waved his wand, pushing a wall of energy at her that bulged in the center. Patsy and Lois joined her and the three combined their magic, pushing the wave back at him.

"This is the end of days for you, Sirius. The ranks of your followers are growing thinner all the time."

Lacey moved fast, running in a zigzag in her gray Clark's sneakers, tossing fireballs in Sirius' direction. Flames struck him hard in the neck and he stumbled, falling over a witch who lay still in the grass, jostling his wand out of his hand. He tumbled into the grass, scrambling to his feet and searching for his wand.

"Not so fast," Lacey cautioned, wagging her finger at him.

"Stupid bitch," he grumbled, diving for his wand and lifting it up, releasing shadows that curled up around him, momentarily hiding him. Sparks flew out from the darkness that was floating out around the knees of Louie and the wizard he was fighting, condensing across the battle-field, dangerously hiding the enemy.

Lois waded forward, waving her wand to blow away the shadows, whipping her head around in surprise. Sirius was nowhere to be found.

"He still has a few good tricks," said Lacey. "That last one was a punch in the gut. Fortunately, he tends to run when things get tough." She looked at Leira, who was running toward her, her face twisted in horror.

Lacey followed Leira's eyes down to her stomach where a crimson stain was spreading in a spidery pattern across her velour top. "That's going to be a problem." She pressed her hand against the wound and dropped to her knees as Leira ran toward her, sliding across the grass to catch Lacey as she fell backward.

Lois pushed her glasses up her nose and ran for her old friend, Patsy helping to clear a path. Lois got to Lacey, pulling the head of the Silver Griffins into her lap and cradling her head. "Lacey, hang in there. Let me try a spell."

But it was too late. Life had already seeped out of her and her body had gone limp. "This has gone too far," snarled Lois, hugging her friend's body close to her chest.

The fighting still raged on around them, Sirius' followers sensing an opening and pressing their advantage. Leira stood up, her eyes narrowed, a smear of blood across her chest.

"Enough!"

"No!" Jackson reached out with his hand, running toward his daughter. But Leira was already letting the energy surge through her, rattling the bracelet on her arm. *End this battle, now!* She clenched her fists, the magic building till it pushed outward in an explosion of light that quickly rippled across the field.

Correk shielded his eyes with his arm, making his way to the last place he saw Leira. The dark magicals turned and ran away from the light, tripping and falling over bodies spread out on the field.

The light pulled at Leira as the bracelet burned against her wrist, easing her anger as it built, drawing her closer. She drifted out of her body as a hand grabbed onto her shoulder, yanking her backwards. Her eyes popped open, a swell of pain passing through her body, leaving a residue in her shoulders.

Hagan was standing in front of her, his meaty hand on her shoulder and a look of concern on his face. "You and I still make a damn good team, kid."

"Lacey," muttered Leira, her eyes gleaming. She blinked back tears as Hagan wrapped his arms around her, squeezing her tight and the grief pushed out some of the light.

Leira suddenly pushed away from him and looked around frantically. "Sirius! Did someone get him?"

"He got clean away," said Lois, leaning against Patsy. "We'll find my brother, if I have to hunt him down myself and drag him to Trevilsom Prison. He'll never see outside those walls again."

Louie and Jackson surrounded the remaining witches and wizards with Yumfuck. Louie threatened them with the sword while the troll swiped a paw through the air, barely missing each time. Jackson sent out a stream of energy that circled around the opposition, forcing them back into an ever tighter clump. Silver Griffins were splitting into two groups, half of them gathering around Lacey Trader to shield her body and the other half rounding up the dark witches and wizards.

An older witch pulled out a long black cloak and laid it on the ground. Two wizards gently lifted her body and placed her on top of the cloak, wrapping her up in it. They lifted her body as a trio of witches opened a large portal and they began to move everyone out of there. Last to go was the group escorting Lacey's body, a wizard cradling her in his arms as the others walked on either side of him.

"I'm going to go with them," said Lois.

"Ditto," said Patsy, helping Lois limp toward the portal, following behind the cortege.

A small group stayed behind, and a tall, round witch came over to Leira and Correk. "You can all go home. We will take care of the dead. This is what we were trained for and we will move faster on our own."

"Leira..." Correk squeezed her hand. "We need to go. You stopped any more bloodshed. We need to take that and get going. There's something we need to do."

"This shouldn't have happened," said Leira.

"You didn't cause it and you couldn't have done any more than you did," said Eireka, trying to smile at her daughter.

"We all fought bravely, none more than Lacey," said Mara. "Go do what you have to do next. Lacey would want it that way. The threat of Wolfstan Humphrey hasn't passed. If anything, it's worse."

"I'll call you," said Eireka, hugging her daughter, surrounding her with her energy. Mara took her granddaughter's hand, doing the same, the three energies combining briefly into one.

"Where are we going?" asked Leira, tilting up her chin to look at Correk.

"To see the Jersey Willen. I'll explain on the way. We're going to take a portal to Enchanted Rock. There's no time."

The troll came plodding over, shaking the ground with his footsteps. He got to Correk and shrank back down to five inches as Correk held out his hand and scooped him up, putting Yumfuck on his shoulder.

Leira gave a weary smile. "I trust you. If you say we need to go, then we're out of here. Hagan, will you be alright?"

"I've got a lot of padding around the frame. I'll be fine. I'll let Harkin and the Gardener know what happened."

"My father won't take it well that he missed the entire fight," said Correk, his face drawn. "But he'll get over it." He held up his hands and created a ball of light, pulling it apart and singing into it. A portal opened and on the other side was the entrance to the kemana and Hillsdale.

Correk stepped through and put out his hand for Leira. She let go of her mother and stepped through looking back at all the people who had been willing to fight by her side as the portal closed. Family.

Leira stepped up onto the Jersey Willen's porch, her mind still going over every detail of the battle, looking for a way to make things turn out differently. Correk tapped lightly on the door, stepping back. He opened his pocket and looked down at Yumfuck. "You stay hidden the entire time. We need to get this over and done so we can go home and... and just sit."

Yumfuck nodded solemnly, making a cross over his heart with his little paw.

A faded lacey curtain moved across the window and the Jersey Willen looked out and saw the pair standing on the porch. His whiskers twitched and he nervously opened the door. "You two look like you've had better days."

"There was a battle," said Leira in a gush of air. She shook her head and said nothing more.

"Sirius came looking for us," said Correk, rubbing his forehead. "Lacey Trader was killed."

The Jersey Willen sucked in air, patting his chest with his paw. A shudder passed through him and jiggled his body, metallic objects in the folds of his skin jangling together.

"Sirius got away," said Correk, "and we think he's looking for the ring on Wolfstan's behalf. We need you to keep it moving, for your sake as well as to keep the ring safe. Do you have any Willens you can trust to protect it and not pawn it?"

"I have a family of hundreds who would be honored. We've never forgotten what you did for us. Say no more and consider it done."

"There's one more favor," said Leira, her throat dry. "We need you to use that same network to look for Sirius. He may only be a pawn in this nightmare but he's a powerful one and he needs to be stopped before anyone else gets hurt. He needs to answer for what he has done."

"We'll pay you, of course. We were thinking mylar blankets. Shiny and practical," said Correk.

The Jersey Willen rubbed his paws together, looking at Correk and Leira on the porch. "I'll let the others know. It will help put more of my brethren on your task."

Leira reached out and rubbed the Jersey Willen's shoulder through his brocade vest. "Thank you for all your help. I'm not sure I've said that enough to you."

The Willen was taken aback and opened and shut his mouth several times, letting out tiny squeaks. Finally, he found his voice. "In all my days, Leira Berens, no one has ever treated me with the respect you have on any given day. It's an honor to help you any time I can. Although a blanket would be nice, too."

CHAPTER TWENTY-ONE

L acey Trader's funeral was planned for two days after her death. It was tradition in the Silver Griffins to not wait any more than forty-eight hours, especially for someone who had led them so valiantly and for so long.

The funeral was held in Chicago behind St. James Episcopal Cathedral around the labyrinth. Beside the labyrinth stood a three foot statue of a famous Arpak with his arms outstretched in sorrow. It also worked well for the human parishioners who mistook him for a saint.

The rector, Reverend Peter Gleason was a boyish looking wizard who had graduated from the Virginia Seminary. He stood patiently in his vestments with his hands folded, waiting for everyone to assemble.

Turner Underwood personally took care of the glamours around the church, using a similar spell as the one he used around the School of Necessary Magic. People wandering down leafy Huron Street suddenly found themselves turning around and walking down North Rush wondering why they were outside at all.

Lacey had been preserved for the forty-eight hours it took to make the necessary arrangements for such a dignitary in the magical world. She was dressed in her favorite sensible skirt and sweater set with a pair of comfortable Clark's on her feet. Her body was floating above a large round basin set up just outside the entrance to the labyrinth. The basin was full of water from the rivers of Rodania brought over by Mara and Jackson.

Silver Griffins were chosen from every region to represent their part of the world along with most of the rank and file from Chicago. Mabel Garner stood in the center of the Chicago contingent, pressed shoulder to shoulder, biting her lower lip and determined not to cry.

The dean of the seminary was there with General Anderson, the only human permitted to be at the ceremony. He had left his uniform at home and was dressed in his best black suit that he hadn't worn since the funeral of Jessica Anderson, and after today he planned to never wear it again.

Lois was there in a black pantsuit with Earl in his one good suit, shiny at the elbows and a new blue silk tie Lois picked out for him just for the day. Lily Sharpton stood next to her aunt, her eyes shining. Inside her pocket was the necklace she had found, but she had yet to say anything, waiting for the right time. *Maybe after the funeral. Maybe I'm wrong and it's nothing.*

Patsy stood next to them quietly chewing on a peanut M&M doing her best to calm her nerves. A wad of tissues was tucked in her sleeve just in case.

Leira stood near the statue with her mother and grandmother, and Jackson and Harkin, while Correk was beside the rector as the new Fixer with Turner Underwood right behind him. Louie stood quietly at the back of the crowd taking it all in.

Correk looked over at Leira, not sure what to do and she gave him a crooked smile wanting to stand closer to him. The troll stirred in her pocket and poked out his head, his paws holding on to the edge of her pocket. The rector held up his hands, his white cassock draping down under his arms. Around his neck was a silk purple stole with an embroidered S and a G intertwined in gold thread.

"Today is an opportunity for reflection," began Reverend Gleason, "not only for the life well-lived of Lacey Trader, but for our own lives and where we see ourselves in them. Lacey Trader saw her place in a life of service from a very young age. She was a gifted witch who looked out for others and had an opinion about everything that she always felt okay about sharing." A sprinkling of laughter rolled across the crowd. "Her ability to change your mind about something you were certain about just minutes ago with just a steady look and an arch of her brow was legendary. I found myself questioning a few things after a chat with Lacey. " The wizard smiled, creases deepening around his eyes. "It was her love of service that lead her to that battlefield in a peaceful place, where most battles are held. It was her love of this world and the magicals that live here that lead her to charge into battle. And it was even her love of human beings, maybe even especially, that lead her to keep going even when the odds were not in her favor. It was never about self-preservation for Lacey Trader, my very good friend..." The rector paused, swallowing hard and wiping away a tear. "It was about love, which is all service really is in the end, one to another without expectation of return. Rest well my friend," said Reverend Gleason, his voice breaking. "You have more than earned it. I will see you again across the veil."

Others stepped forward to talk about their fondest memory of Lacey, evoking tears and laughter. After a while the Reverend stepped up again and raised his hands. "We would like to end with a few words from one of Lacey's greatest and oldest friends, and the new head of the Silver Griffins."

Lois stepped forward as a murmur rose but was silenced with one look from Turner Underwood. Lois stood up straighter and said, "I am honored to be called to serve this institution. And I am humbled to be following in the footsteps of Lacey Trader. We were in more than a few battles together back in the day and the subject of death occasionally came up between us. Lacey was fond of quoting Winston Churchill when it did. She would say, I am ready to meet my Maker. Whether my Maker is prepared for the great ordeal of meeting me is another matter. Churchill and Lacey were great friends and fought side by side in the war. I imagine they're back to swapping tall tales already."

Harkin smiled, surprised to find himself comforted to be surrounded by family. Several Silver Griffins made note of his presence, but no one would disrespect the solemnity of the occasion by bringing up the death of Fraekin. It could wait till another day. Harkin looked over the crowd and narrowed his gaze when he saw Agent Erickson standing near him. He took a step forward and put out his hand to make the first move. "I don't know if you remember me."

"Harkin, I know who you are," said Erickson, pressing his lips together.

"Of course. I knew your mother. She was a great Silver Griffin at Trevilsom Prison. I was sorry to hear of her passing."

Erickson looked down at his shoes covered in dew around the toes and back at Harkin. "Thank you," he said clearing his throat.

"I'm sure she would be so proud to see what you're doing with the Silver Griffins in her place. You're in the leadership. Well done."

Erickson blanched, his eyes widening, and he shook his head vigorously. "Excuse me," he said, digging his way to the back of the crowd to stand next to Xander Powell, a representative from Virginia.

"It's time," said the rector, raising his arms.

Everyone took a step back and made a clearing for the Reverend, Lois, Correk and Turner Underwood to pass through with Lacey's body floating between them. The Reverend whispered something too faint to hear and the water from the basin rose up, surrounding Lacey's body in a watery bubble, accompanying her on the last part of her journey.

Correk nodded to Leira and reached out his hand to her and Eireka gave her a nudge to go join them. The troll dropped out of her pocket and Mara scooped him up, placing him on her shoulder. Leira went over to walk behind the body as they wove their way around to the center of the labyrinth and out again, repeating an ancient blessing. "Safe travels with friends to guide you, till we meet again. Rest easy, with joy and laughter, knowing all is well, at last."

The small group entered the cathedral from a side door going down the aisle, passing through the narthex, repeating the blessing till they went behind the sanctuary to the stone wall covered in marble tile. Here the rector pressed his hand against the stone, his hand glowing as a door appeared. He pressed a little harder and the door slid into the wall, stone scraping loudly against cement. Cobwebs covered part of the passageway as they all filed quietly inside and Correk threw a ball of light gently above them to light the way. In front of them were twisting stone steps that lead further and further underground, turning and turning, lit only by the ball of light above them.

Leira felt the hum of energy increase the deeper they went underground, passing by walls made of stone bricks until finally they came to a tall metal door. The Reverend stopped and turned to face Lacey's cortege.

"I feel like something should be said before we pass through this door. It's been years since we've had occasion to enter the Catacombs of Derry. Even though they've been here for thousands of years, very few are ever laid to rest here. Lacey Trader is more than worthy of this honor to lay among the revered from the magical world. Not because of the post she held, but what was in her heart." He nodded to Turner Underwood who came forward with an oversized key, placing it in the lock and turning it. *Tink, tink, tink, click.* The tumblers turned over, unlocking the door. Correk, Turner and the Reverend pushed together, putting their backs into it to get the great door to swing wide with a loud creak that sounded more like a moan.

A rush of energy poured out, surrounding all of them and creating ripples along the water surrounding Lacey's body. Leira felt the magic rise in her, making her feel light headed as she followed everyone through the door and onto a terrace that overlooked a circular system of hundreds of terraces stacked one on top of the other that looked more like the inside of an enormous beehive. The opening in the center stretched across for hundreds of feet.

Each terrace that went all the way around the opening had a series of doors every few yards. And all of it looked down over a center courtyard with an even larger basin full of the same water.

Placed on shelves here and there around the wide opening, and flush with the walls were bodies wrapped in purple silk. Leira's eyes widened and her eyes glowed from the magic floating through the room. "It's a kind of artifact," whispered Leira. "All this magic is resting here."

"These catacombs connect all the world. Those doors go to Madrid, and Senegal, and London, and Beirut, and even Cleveland," said the Reverend with a smile. "This is a magical plane created thousands of years ago that will only ever be seen by a few living magicals each generation."

The group walked halfway around the terrace, stopping at an empty space. Lois and Reverend Gleason stood to the far side of the empty shelf as Turner and Correk stepped back, Correk putting his arm around Leira. The water swirled around Lacey's body, suddenly churning faster and faster, weaving the same purple cloth that was covering the other bodies laid to rest in the catacombs. Her shrouded body floated within the churning water toward the shelf finally coming to rest as the water pulled itself away, swirling first around Lois and then climbing to the center of the open space before diving down into the eternal basin at the bottom.

"The waters have acknowledged the new choice for the head of the Silver Griffins, Lois. The ceremony is complete." The Reverend put a hand on Lacey's shroud. "Goodbye old friend."

Each one took their turn saying goodbye before following in a line out of the catacombs and back through the door. Correk and the Reverend and Turner pulled it shut with the same loud scraping, the door locking on its own. They made their way quietly back up the long set of stairs, Correk holding Leira's hand and passing down the middle aisle, to the outside courtyard.

The area had already been transformed with tables covered in white linen and trays full of ham biscuits and pickled peaches and pickled watermelon and sandwiches from a nearby deli. All Lacey's favorites. People had glasses of champagne in their hands and were telling stories about Lacey, smiling and laughing and saying hello to old faces they hadn't seen in a while.

The troll went over to Leira with his arms out and she scooped him up so he could kiss her on the cheek and hug her face. "Thank you, my furry friend. Go find something to eat. I know you're hungry and from the lack of mayhem I know you've been on your very best behavior. Go get a sandwich. It's okay."

"Yeah?"

"Yeah," she said, putting him back on the ground. He

disappeared into the crowd, climbing onto a table and it wasn't long before a sandwich was bobbling up and down on a tray, walking away seemingly on its own.

Leira and Correk made their way through the crowd together, saying hello to General Anderson and hugging Lois and Patsy, meeting Earl. It took a while to greet everyone, but finally Leira looked at Correk and let out a weary sigh. "Let's take the train home. I need to be alone with you and Yumfuck for a while. I think we've greeted everyone by now."

"You're with the Fixer. Let's travel through a portal this time." Correk found the troll buried in a bowl of olives, wearing one on each arm and nibbling at the edges. He scooped him up with his olives and wrapped him in a napkin, putting him in his pocket. He took Leira's hand and they walked into a small side courtyard outside of the glamour but hidden by church walls on all sides. A ball of light grew in his hands and he pulled it apart, opening up a portal to their kitchen in DC. Leira stepped through first, heading for the back porch, shedding her shoes as she walked. Correk followed, closing the portal with sparks dancing around the kitchen floor. He went to the refrigerator and got out two long necked beers and walked out to the porch, opening them and handing one to Leira. There they sat in silence, holding hands and sipping their beers long into the night.

CHAPTER TWENTY-TWO

The heat was rising as the morning grew later. It had been a day and a night since Lacey was laid to rest and everyone had walked around the house, saying very little and eating less.

Yumfuck woke up when the sun hit his face and spent the morning meditating, wondering how to change things. "First, leave this room." The troll grabbed his favorite Batman backpack out of the closet, searching the front pocket for the twenty dollar bill Hagan had slipped him before they left the sanctuary. This time he was going to pay for his donuts. His stash was empty and Correk had been in no mood to replenish his own. He needed to get out and find something to do. "I have been sitting still long enough."

He crept down the stairs of the quiet house and down the hallway to the kitchen, pressing his face to the screen door. Leira was sitting on the back porch with a beer, gazing over the alley and occasionally letting out a long sigh. Correk had left to help a magical in trouble somewhere in Little Rock, Arkansas. He had checked in on Yumfuck before he left, barely saying anything.

"We need a little joy to come back in here," muttered Yumfuck, heading back down the hall. "I've got to go find some."

He shoved the large wooden front door open, squeezing one eye shut when it creaked and waiting to see if Leira got up to come and check on the noise. Nothing. "That's not good." His stomach rumbled and he rubbed it, licking his lips. "This mood is making me hungry."

He jumped up and down, trying to reach the handle without success. He went to the edge of the steps and looked up and down the street. Even the street was quiet. The troll went back to the door and grew to three feet to pull it tight before shrinking back down, dropping off the front steps into the bushes, crossing from yard to yard without being seen.

The aroma of someone cooking dinner floated out of a window and he stopped to breathe in deeply, feeling himself relax. He looked at the open window and thought about going inside, just for a minute, but thought better of it.

"I'm on a mission. There has to be a way to help."

He walked for blocks but wasn't finding anything that could help and there was no donut shop in sight. The day was not getting any better. He found a small park and wandered into it, crawling up onto a bench and sitting back on one of the slats. He slumped back and let out a sigh and a squeak.

"It doesn't sound like things are working out for you

today," said an old man, startling the troll. Yumfuck sat up straighter, ready to drop down and find cover before anyone could pull out a phone. He watched the old man feel for the edge of the seat with his hand, holding on to his cane as he sat down hard, falling back onto the bench and smiling, satisfied.

"I hope you don't mind if an old blind man takes up some of your space. This is my favorite place to sit too." The man lifted his face to the warmth of the sun, a breeze lifting the few hairs still left on his head. The man's forehead wrinkled, and he tilted his head toward Yumfuck. "Cat got your tongue?"

Yumfuck stuck out his tongue, feeling it with his paw. "No, it's still right here," he said, still holding onto his tongue.

The old man chuckled, slapping his knee. "You sound like a young one. How can things be so dire for someone so young?"

"I'm a lot older than you think and things have not been going well lately. An old friend was killed."

"Oooh, that is tough," he said, wincing. "I've always thought it was the loss of the little things that hurt the most when a friend dies. Having coffee with them or expecting to hear their voice when you go to work."

The troll let out a sigh and crossed his paws over his belly. "When does the sadness go away?"

"Son, that is a question without an answer. Grief is something we all want to avoid, but it's really the balm we need. It's there to help us remember what we love about the one we lost and to take it in even deeper. But how long it takes varies and it will probably come for a visit, and

MARTHA CARR & MICHAEL ANDERLE

then leave for a while, only to return later to help open your heart again, just a little bit more."

"I need to get on with things. I can't wait for grief to be done with me."

The old man nodded his head. "Too true. Life goes marching forward all the time. That is another one of the blessings. We can put ourselves back into the flow of life and let it carry us for a while, like a river. We go about our day, we get things done and in the background, grief still talks to us, reminding us that we were loved, and therefore, we will be again."

"Going back to life for my family is not so easy. Trouble has our address and keeps knocking at our door."

"When trouble has found you, invite it in as a friend and ask, what are you here to teach me."

"I'm not sure that will work in this case. We've put up all kinds of things to make sure trouble stays outside."

"I suppose you mean the walking, talking kind of trouble, and I mean the kind that poisons you from the inside out. If you want to defeat the first one, learn to master the second one."

Yumfuck's stomach rumbled and he stood up on the bench. "I think I actually feel a little better."

"Then I was of service to someone today and that makes me glad."

The troll was about to jump off the bench and stopped. "I don't suppose you know where there's a decent donut shop nearby."

"As a matter of fact, I do, and I was having the same thought. Do you mind some company?"

"Not at all, and don't worry, I can pay for myself this time."

The man laughed and stood up, gathering his cane. "Follow me. I'm not too fast. Hope that's not a problem."

"No, today I have time."

"You're a little fella, aren't you?"

"Depends on the day."

"Now that's a good riddle. I like riddles," he said as they made their way down the street toward a line of shops. "I am not alive, but I grow. I don't have lungs, but I need air. I don't have a mouth, but water kills me. What am I? Give up? Fire!"

A man passed the odd pair, looking down at the furry creature walking next to the old man. Yumfuck looked up at him and smiled, waving his tiny paw. The man shook his head, taking another look and pressed his hand to his stomach as he kept walking. "My wife is right, for once. Enough Taco Bell and you start to see things."

They ambled to the next block and came to a stop in front of Square Donuts. The old man went to open the door and Yumfuck pulled on his pant leg. "I'm gonna wait out here. Here's my twenty," he said, slipping it out of his backpack. He jumped up onto the cement ledge under the window, holding it up as high as he could. "A dozen assorted, a few with cream filling, please."

The man put out his hand and Yumfuck waved it near him till he found it and folded the money into his hand. "Will do. Shouldn't be long." He opened the door and went in, the owner yelling out a greeting that was lost as soon as the door swung shut. Yumfuck pressed his little face against the window, watching the old man make his way carefully toward the counter. A woman at a nearby table let out a yelp and jumped out of her chair, pointing to Yumfuck and waving to her friend.

Yumfuck waved, giving her a wink. Her eyes grew wide and she opened and shut her mouth like a fish. Yumfuck laughed and imitated her, waving to her friend. The pair came closer just as the old man came out of the shop carrying two boxes. "They're still warm," said the old man. "Perfect time of day to come here. I have a little change for you too."

"Keep the change," said Yumfuck holding up his arms as the man held the box out for him, balancing it on his furry little head. "I'm paying it forward."

He neatly jumped down, walking alongside his new friend, making his way back toward home. "Do you come to that bench often?"

"Most days, around the same time. You thinking of joining me again?"

"I'm thinking that is one of the best ideas I've had in a while," said Yumfuck, feeling the ache ease just a little. Grief would have to come back and visit on another day.

Louie gripped the sword, standing barefoot in the center of the space he had cleared in his small apartment. "Big enough."

He closed his eyes and took a deep breath, trying to connect with the energy of the sword. It was helping to take his mind off the battle in Texas. He was tired of closing his eyes and watching it all unfold over and over again.

He felt the handle of the sword hum in his hands and the energy grow stronger. He tightened his grip on the handle as the artifacts he had collected shook in their boxes. *Patience,* whispered the sword.

Just as he was about to swing the sword, tired of waiting for direction, there was a knock on the door. "Weird how you can do that," he muttered, holding the sword in one hand and walking over to look through the peephole. "Ava," he whispered, breathlessly.

Her long black hair was pulled back at the nape of her neck and she wore a white t-shirt and a pair of black jeans and boots.

"Hey!" She smiled, leaning toward the peephole. "Can I come in?"

Louie looked around at the pile of dirty clothes and the empty cartons from the restaurant downstairs. "Hang on, one second!" He grabbed the sword and ran to the narrow closet, shoving it inside, behind the coats. "Sorry friend, I'll put you in your case later." He hurriedly scooped up the clothes, puckering his lips from the smell and turning away his face. He ran into his small bedroom and dropped the clothes, kicking them under his bed.

Ava tapped lightly on the door again. "Louie? Are you coming?"

"Yeah, I'm coming." He shoved the empty cartons in the packed trash can, putting the forks into the sink and spun around looking at the room. "Not too bad," he said, jogging over to the door and pulling it open.

Ava smiled and came in, looking around at the apartment. "How bad was it?" She pulled her bag off her shoulder, setting it on the round table in the room.

"About three days' worth of buildup. Medium bad." He rubbed the back of his head, sheepishly. "What can I do for you?"

Ava's face warmed and she dug her hands in her pocket. "I... I uh... I was just looking to hang out, you know, get to know you better."

Louie's grin spread across his face, his dimples showing. "My charm is finally getting to you. Yeah, sure. My house is practically your house, and you're always welcome." He stopped talking, at a loss for words as he caught himself watching how she moved. He cleared his throat, desperately searching for a topic as the silence grew more awkward. "Did you work today?" he finally asked. *Get a grip. You never have this much trouble around a girl.*

"No, Dad had enough help today and I had lessons."

"Oh yeah? How's the parkour lessons going?" *Okay, found a topic.*

"I managed to get across the first obstacle course, but I kissed it on the second one." She rolled up part of her sleeve and showed him the purple and green bruise blossoming on her shoulder. "So really well," she said with a laugh. "I think I'm the only one who hasn't broken anything yet."

"Tell me again why you're taking parkour?"

"Dad said a young woman has to know how to defend herself and I made a pretty good argument that getting away was even more important." She found a seat on a bar stool and cautiously rested her elbow, lifting it back up again when it stuck to the counter.

"Sorry about that. I must have missed a spot," said Louie, wiping the counter vigorously in front of Ava.

"It's okay, my room doesn't look much better. Full disclosure." Her face warmed and she ducked her chin.

She is cute. How did I miss that? Louie smiled and grabbed two sodas from the fridge, handing one to her. She looked at the label. "I'm impressed. You got the real thing."

"I was feeling rich today," he laughed. "I bought real Coke this time instead of orange Fanta. I'm living high on the hog."

"Hey, I love orange soda. That and a hot dog and I'm good to go."

"What do you put on your dog?"

Ava waved her hand. "Nothing. I like it on a bun, nothing added."

"Heresy! You gotta do it up right. Mustard and relish. No ketchup, worse than plain."

"Got it," said Ava. "But I'm standing by my plain. Although," she chirped, pointing a finger at the ceiling, "when I was younger, I used to mash potato chips under the dog."

"Doubling up on the carbs with a little added grease. I can respect that. All you needed was some liquid cheese on top."

"Nooooo!" she laughed, waving her hands.

Louie grinned again and leaned back against the counter, feeling his shirt stick and doing his best to ignore it. And without even noticing that for just a little while, he forgot about everything else.

Sirius slammed his fist on the oak table. "I am the head of this family," he screamed.

"Past tense, you *were*." Agnes was yelling just as loudly. "You left, remember?"

They were standing in the sitting room of the family estate in Kentucky. Outside in the hallway, witches and wizards passed by the doors, flinching at the sound of something crashing or Sirius' deep voice carrying out to them. Opinion was mixed on who they wanted to see win the argument.

"You left to become Wolfstan Humphrey's handmaiden," said Agnes, spitting out the words. "Tell me you haven't become so stupid that you think you're his partner?"

"I made a necessary and temporary deal," hissed Sirius. "Leira Berens will be the end of the Dark Families, sooner rather than later. Our efforts have failed, over and over again. We needed a powerful ally."

Agnes clenched her fists. "Stop lying. You had no choice but to make the deal and with an Elf," she said, her lip curling. "An ex con from Trevilsom Prison, no less." She shook her head. "He can destroy you, and you know it. You're a fool, Sirius and the worst kind. You're doing someone else's bidding and you'll never get what you want in the bargain."

"Let's talk about delusions and stupidity, Agnes," growled Sirius menacingly. "You sent children out to play with the furry beasts with fangs. No training, no back up and you got some of them killed. Mauled by shifters."

"That you created!" A vein pulsed in Agnes' forehead.

"We created." His voice grew calmer, steadier. It was one of his best attributes that when cornered Sirius started to see the angles. Agnes didn't. "You overplayed your hand without a real plan of action. At least I have a destination, even if there's been a few hiccups."

"You killed the head of the Silver Griffins. You brought hell down on all of us," said Agnes, throwing a book at Sirius' head. He ducked easily, letting it skitter across the floor behind him. "You ended our peaceful reign of mutually ignoring each other. Now, it's not just Leira Berens who wants us gone, it's thousands of our own kind! Our own cousins! Your sister is their new leader." She began pacing around a settee. "I don't know, maybe if I hand them your head and promise we burned the rest of you they'll go back to leaving us to our own devices."

Sirius arched an eyebrow. "I'd like to see you try."

"So would I, and someday it may come to that." Agnes stopped pacing. "Be careful, Sirius. You are losing every ally you once had and someday you may find yourself alone with Wolfstan Humphrey and his gruesome plot and he may suddenly see you in a different light."

"I've got him handled. And I'll get my seat back in the family."

"Your time here has passed. Move on, Sirius and find a dark hole to crawl into and retire."

"Not while Leira Berens lives. Everything was working out the way we planned for generations till that bitch showed up."

"Finally, something we still agree on, but that's the only thing. And no, we don't need your help to take her out. You've done too much already."

CHAPTER TWENTY-THREE

Turner Underwood went running down the hall of his house, not even bothering to tap his cane. He passed by his library as the old King of Oriceran looked up from an ancient tome, pulled out of his memories. "Where are you going in such a hurry?"

"Lucius is on the hunt. He's determined to avenge the stupidity of the Dark Families. I'm afraid they have no idea what they've unleashed and won't see it coming."

The King wandered into the hallway, picking up his pace to keep up with Turner. "How do you redress stupidity? He would have to kill them all. Ah, I see your point."

Turner ran back the way he had come, passing by the king and stepping into his library, stopping for a moment in the middle of the room, rubbing his chin. "Where is that..."

"Now what's happening?" The king turned around, waiting in the hallway.

Turner went to the library ladder and climbed to the high shelf, pushing himself along hurriedly. "Got you," he said, pulling out a thin book that was barely holding together. He held it tightly in his hand, climbing down the ladder and moving swiftly in the direction he had been headed. "Lucius will not be easy to stop. He possesses ancient dark magic courtesy of Rhazdon and he is a Light Elf who was powerful before stepping into the world in between."

"And he's a shifter. Why stop him at all?"

Turner turned and looked at the king in surprise. "You know my oath. I'm obligated to help *all* magicals on this world. I don't get to pick and choose." Turner went to a cabinet in his kitchen and opened it, scanning the rows of apothecary jars, stacked one on top of the other. "Yeah, this is good. Maybe this will slow him down," he muttered. He slipped the jar of dried Oriceran Baylean leaves into his coat pocket and picked up his Homburg off the kitchen table, securing it squarely on his head. "I'm off," he said. "You have the run of the house. The fridge is full, and I just added Apple TV."

"Not so fast, you old Elf. I'm going with you." The king opened the coat closet, pulling out his old battle sword he had brought from the world in between. "It was the only place I could find to put it out of the way. I don't want to be a rude guest."

"Then next time clean off the old blood. There's rags under the sink." Turner tapped his cane twice on the ground, letting out a high pitched whistle, the air shimmering in front of him, thinning out till a portal opened to the Dark Family estate in Kentucky. "And you're older than I am," he said, stepping through.

A howl went up in the distance, answered by a long

series of yips and howls. "Looks like we're a little late to this party," said the king, holding up his tall broadsword. "It's been a long time since I've been in a good battle," he said, his pulse racing.

"We're here to diminish the carnage, not create it. I'm a peacekeeper first, old friend." Turner listened for the next series of howls and call backs. "That's not Lucius. He's not here yet. Those shifters are doing his bidding, gathering the packs in the area. This is not good." Turner waved his cane over his head, disappearing and reappearing across the field.

The king rolled his eyes in frustration and took off at a run to keep up. They were well into the trees before he was on Turner's heels. "I had forgotten about your old tricks. I still don't see why you don't let a few of the Dark Family fall. From what you said, they're hunting your protege. This would solve that thorny problem."

"The old guard sent their offspring to do their dirty work. Mere children who don't know any better. Some of whom may choose differently and leave dark magic behind if given a chance. Lucius is about to take away that chance and despite what some may think, he's not evil. But he will have to live with the choices he makes today, and he bears enough of a burden."

"Why haven't you called your protege to help? Where is Leira Berens?"

"Her presence could make this whole thing blow up. The Dark Families would think there was an opportunity and come out with everything they had…"

"Playing right into Lucius' hands. Excellent point. But

you can't let the families keep harming others and then rescuing them when there are consequences."

"I am not that foolish. There will be consequences, but let it be at their own hands."

"You always did like speaking in riddles," said the king.

The ground began to shake beneath their feet and Turner held up his hand to silence the king. Finally, he heard the sound he had been waiting for that told him Lucius had arrived and was running with his pack. A roar that sounded more like a lion than a wolf, ending in a howl.

Doors could be seen opening along the large house and figures running from the barn toward the open field. The king watched them pile out in small numbers and shrugged at Turner. "You may be wrong. You may not be able to save stupid. It appears they're about to bring a knife to a gunfight."

The howling picked up, with intermittent yipping answering back and forth. "Do you hear that?" asked Turner, pulling out the jar in his pocket. "They're relaying orders."

"Lucius has not forgotten his training as a soldier and has come armed with a plan. I'm the one who trained him. No matter what you do, there will be some who get through. Lucius was the best student I ever had."

"There's no need to be proud."

"There's every reason. Every kingdom, every nation likes to think they're kind and generous but there's always someone who wants more and if there were no soldiers, they would take it. Lucius is here to show them that they can't. It's exactly what these entitled magical imposters need. They believe they should rule, let them prove it."

"Why did you come again?"

"Because you are both my friends and I will fight by your sides every time I am called."

The yipping and howling continued, growing closer.

"I don't remember calling you."

"It was understood." The king strapped the sword by his side, his eyes glowing. "I won't harm Lucius or his pack unless they strike at you or me first. But I will try to dissuade them by other means. Lucius is not the only one who learned a few things in the world in between."

There was a sharp howl that ended on a high note as the ground rumbled again but this time without pause. The shifters appeared at the edge of the trees, with a large wolf leading the pack. "Lucius," whispered Turner, taking out a pinch of the powder and blowing it into the air.

Lucius lifted his snout and snapped his head to the right, glaring at Turner and curling his lip, baring his fangs. He looked over at the old king and seemed to hesitate, his pack howling and yipping behind him. The old king lifted his chin, standing up straighter and finally gave a nod to Lucius.

"You're not helping," said Turner, annoyed, swinging his cane over his head and disappearing again. The king looked around for signs of the old Fixer and it took him a moment but he finally spotted him down by the house, standing in front of the witches and wizards, facing the shifters who were crowding the top of the curving pasture.

"Old fool," hissed the king, brandishing his sword to run to the middle of the field. "An oath's an oath. "Tonight we fight with honor and to the end," he screamed, lifting his sword high in the air and howling as loud as he could, throwing back his head, his long hair cascading down his back.

Lucius stood up on his back legs, lifting his large head and howling in return to his old friend.

Turner rolled his eyes, carefully pulling out the book he had brought with him. "The old guard does love their theatrics." He opened the book, careful not to rip the yellowing paper. Words appeared as he leafed through it, disappearing as he gently turned the page. "Here it is, at last." He wet his dry lips and held up his large hand, raising it high in the air. "Clear as glass, strong as steel. By my word. Quoniam iuramentum meum. Make it so."

The witches and wizards around him hesitated, waiting for something to shimmer or burn or fly through the air. But nothing happened. They looked at the old Fixer, puzzled for only a moment, surprised that he was standing still and not trying to get out of the way.

Lucius fell back down on all four paws and began to run, picking up speed as he came down the hill, flanked by the largest wolves of the pack, the others spreading out behind them to the left and to the right.

They made a V pattern around the old King of Oriceran who whooped and hollered, waving his sword over his head at the thundering paws passing within inches of him, so close he could feel their heated breath as they ran down the hill.

A witch raised her wand, aiming it at the weaker right side and threw a long line of blue flame, her mouth forming an 'O' when the fire hit an invisible wall and bounced back, hitting her squarely in the chest, knocking her to the ground and burning her flesh.

The king watched the other witches and wizards hesitate, looking at each other and not sure what to do. "Ah yes, consequences of their own actions. You are a clever one, Turner Underwood. Sometimes the lessons an old Fixer doles out are harsh."

Lucius stopped short of the glamour the Fixer had built, lifting his snout and smelling the air. He pawed at the ground, opening his wide mouth and growling at the witches and wizards only yards from where he stood. Some of the wolves ran headlong into the glamour only to be thrown backward, hitting the ground dazed and stumbling back to their feet.

"Let them in," yelled a wizard, holding up his wand with a shaking hand.

"If you insist," said Turner, raising his hand high in the air again.

A young witch swung her wand around and pulsed energy at the wizard, knocking the air out of him and bringing him to his knees. "He doesn't speak for us. Throw him out there if he's dying to be torn apart by them." The witch stepped closer to the glamour and put her palm against it, flattening her hand. "I'm sorry," she yelled. "I was wrong."

"Coward!" Agnes appeared in the doorway of the house, her wand aimed at the young witch. "We never back down and we definitely never apologize to our enemy." She whipped her wand up and down, a vine of gold sparks winding its way toward the witch.

But to everyone's surprise, her target was ready for her.

The witch twirled her wand in a tight circle, swirling the vine over her head and with an overhand pitch, sent it back to its owner, the thorns digging into Agnes' flesh.

"Listen up, bitch," said the witch. "My name is Ariana and I've had enough of all of you old bags of bones. The Old Guard. We're not doing your dirty work for you anymore. You want to carry on these petty feuds, you do it yourself." The witch raised her wand, creating a wind that moved along the field, her long dark hair swirling above her head. "We are taking over from here. This is our land now and we will align ourselves with magicals. All magicals," she shouted, "including shifters."

Turner Underwood watched with a growing sense of unease even though the wolves were calming down, lining up in rows behind Lucius with only an occasional growl.

"The other leaders will never let this stand," screamed Agnes, twisting in the vines and only making them burrow deeper. Blood was beginning to trickle from her mouth.

"We don't plan to give them a choice," said Ariana. "All this time you've been bickering with each other, arguing over who gets to sit where at that overgrown table. Want to know what we've been doing? Training, day and night. Thank you for setting that up for us, Agnes," she said, a sly smile growing across her face. "We've been forming alliances with other members of the families. Younger members. We were waiting for the right moment. It looks like it's here. Tonight, things change." She nodded to another witch. "Put out the call. We are taking the reins, and nothing is ever going to be the same." She looked at Turner with a cold stare. "Let down your glamour. There's no battle left here. The shifters are our allies and we will fight together."

"Who do you plan to fight, Ariana," said Turner, already suspecting the answer.

"Anyone who tries to harm magicals, of course."

Turner felt a chill go down his spine as he raised his arm and let the glamour fade away. Some of the wolves returned to growling and pawing at the ground, but Lucius barked at them, and they whined and fled to the back of the pack.

The king made his way through the rolling masses of fur and muscle, making his way over to Turner Underwood. "You got what you wanted. There was almost no bloodshed."

"This is worse," said Turner, scowling. "This is much worse. We missed what was really happening with the Dark Families. It looked like there was internecine fighting going on, but that was only the surface. Underneath a new regime was building and they will not be willing to hide in the shadows away from the humans, content to rule their small part of the world. Darkness is coming and the question may turn out to be who it will be coming from. Wolfstan Humphrey and his Frankenstein army or the new leaders of the Dark Families and their poisonous alliances."

CHAPTER TWENTY-FOUR

C orrek stood in an alley on Crowne Oaks Circle in Winston Salem, North Carolina, looking at the apartment window above him. "Bryce Mallory, thirteen, wizard. This should be the place." He double checked the coordinates and tuned into the streams of magic passing by him all the time. The young wizard was still up there.

He walked over and pulled down the fire escape ladder and ran up the steps, two at a time, his boots making almost no noise. He ran past an apartment with a couple inside, giggling and touching each other's arm over two plates of pasta. "First date, maybe second," he muttered, still climbing.

On another floor a girl was holding her hairbrush like a microphone, singing and dancing around her room. Correk kept going, picking up speed, feeling the panic rising in the tween wizard who was still up one more flight.

He got to the metal landing outside the young wizard's

bedroom window and paused, knitting his brows together, feeling a drop in the wizard's energy level. Correk carefully tapped at the frame of the window, the ancient spell he learned turning the lock and lifting the glass. He climbed through, pushing back the curtains and saw the boy curled up in a heap next to an Oriceran conjuring wheel and an oak wand. Tan leather suitcases and a trunk sat neatly just behind the wheel, already packed and waiting for a trip.

Correk stepped into the room and purposefully tended to the young wizard, rolling Bryce onto his side with his legs stretched out and his mouth open. Almost all the wheel's arrows had stopped on a spell to increase magical agility. One was pointing at magical creativity and the tip of the arrow had bent in, leaving a scratch in the wood.

Correk gingerly picked up the wheel as it jerked in his hands, pulling to the right. "You're an artifact," Correk exclaimed, examining it more closely. He pulled out a velvet bag charmed for just these occasions and slid the lurching wheel inside, pulling the drawstring tight and tying them in a knot.

Bryce coughed suddenly, a green gaseous cloud floating out of his mouth that smelled of rotten fruit. Correk knelt on one knee and hovered his hands just above the boy's chest and watched the stream of magic that appeared in front of him. There were dark spots floating here and there in the young wizard's magic stream, disrupting his innate magic and causing it to turn on the boy and attack him.

The new Fixer was about to turn away for a moment to consult a book he had brought with him when something caught his eye. He looked back at the stream, his eyes widening as he realized where he had seen those same markings before. "Lucius."

He dipped his hand into the stream and felt the slight burn, pulling back. It was the mark of the world in between infecting the boy's magic like a virus. Correk scanned the body again as the boy convulsed, the green gas bubbling out of his mouth. He pulled out the book, scanning the words as they appeared on the page, hoping to find something on the world in between.

"Nothing," he spit out, frustrated. He remembered something Turner Underwood had told him more than once when he was first training. *There will be times when nothing is simple, and you don't know what spell to choose. That is when you will need to tune into your own instincts and trust that something is guiding you.*

Correk took a deep breath and tried the easiest spell he knew for removing dark magic. The dark spots shimmered for a moment but quickly returned to their static state and even seemed to be a little bigger. He pressed his lips together, flexing his hands and tried again with a more powerful spell that came with the potential drawback of damaging the boy's magic. Nothing, but no harm to Bryce either. Correk let out the breath he was holding but could feel the time inching by and the danger growing.

"Wait, this is different than normal dark magic. Time *is* the difference. It comes from a place without time." Correk flipped through the book and found it on the next to last page. "To Place an Object on a Different Plane and Remain the Same." The words spilled down the page, explaining how to freeze the virus in place and take away the element of time, but not remove it. "Best used with solid objects," he read, closing the book. "Well, not this time. Trust my own instincts," he muttered. "Here we go." He spread his fingers wide and curled them into fists, opening them again and following the instructions to the letter. Energy flowed through his body, his hands glowing as he moved his hands through the stream of magic, this time, swirling it in a counter-clockwise direction.

"Aperi ianuam. Creare spatium." The inky dark spaces flipped in on themselves swirling in the same direction and shrinking down until they disappeared with a pop. "Secure aternam." Correk watched the flow of magic restore itself and the teenager stir, his legs jerking as the magic inside of him continued to heal.

Correk sat back on his heels and waited for Bryce to regain consciousness, blinking his eyes and groaning as the young wizard stretched out his arms and legs. "What happened?"

"You were very sick," said Correk.

The boy startled and shook his head trying to clear his mind. "You're the Fixer! I was rescued by the Fixer! You're real!"

"Who gave you that conjurer's wheel?"

Bryce pushed himself up on one elbow, his face warming. "I traded for it at school with another magical. I gave him my baseball card collection. He said it had been in his family for a long time and would help me become more powerful."

Correk helped him to sit up. "He was telling you the truth, but it shouldn't be in anyone's hands. You came close to being pulled into the world in between."

The boy turned ashen, hunching his shoulders and

ducking as if something had suddenly swung at him. He swallowed hard and his eyes glistened. "I just wanted to be more powerful. I'm supposed to be going to a new school for magicals and I know almost nothing. I didn't want to look stupid."

Bryce tried to stand, almost falling back as Correk caught him, helping him to sit down in a chair.

"This time things had a happy ending. That won't always be the case." He lifted a tag on the trunk and smiled when he saw, School of Necessary Magic. "You're going to be okay. I know the new headmistress of this place. Her name is Mara Berens and she has a pretty good sense of humor and knows how to help a kid navigate the world."

Bryce let out a shudder, the color returning to his face.

"Bryce, there's a lot of time for you to grow stronger as a wizard. Be patient, try and ask more questions, and trust that you'll learn what you need to know. It won't hurt if you have some fun while you're at it."

"I'm really sorry for all this trouble. Do you have to tell my parents? I'm supposed to be going to a going away party and they will ground me till I leave for school if they find out."

Correk rubbed the back of his head and raised his brows. "No, not this time. We can keep this between us, but I'll give you a little piece of advice about Mara. She doesn't abide by anyone keeping things from her, but she'll fight till the end for someone who's doing the best they can."

Bryce let out a sigh and rubbed his face. "I lost my baseball card collection."

Correk took a few pintas out of his pocket. "When you

get to school you can use these to start a new collection of Louper cards. You'll see, it's a lot cooler game."

"I met the Fixer," whispered Bryce. "You're like a superhero."

"So I've been told."

CHAPTER TWENTY-FIVE

Wolfstan Humphrey sat at his desk, stewing over who could have taken the necklace. What really bothered him was how close they came into his inner sanctum and left no trail. "Magicals," he snarled. "Leira Berens," he spit out. "Witches."

Nothing was going the way he wanted. He ran the list through his head again and again. Harkin was still free. There was dissension and gossip among the corporations that made up the alliance Fleeker had so carefully crafted to trade in Oriceran goods. He ticked the annoyances off on his fingers.

The Dark Families are falling apart and can't be trusted, and Sirius is useless. He shook his head, his lip curling in rage. *Leira Berens lives.* "And someone stole from me," he shouted, bringing his fist down on his desk, rattling it against the floor.

His assistant came all the way to the door and saw the dark mood his boss was in, turned and quietly crept back down the hall. It wasn't worth it.

Wolfstan stood at the window in his office at Fleeker watching employees come and go, letting the hours pass, running the problem through his head. His assistant braved a second try lightly tapping on the door but Wolfstan gave a flick of his wrist without bothering to turn around and the aide fled, grateful to have gotten off so easily.

Finally, a smile that was more of a leer settled on his face. "First the traitor." He let out a satisfied sigh, linking his hands behind his back. "I'm overthinking it. There's a traitor somewhere within these walls who's watching me. Let them find something. I'll trap them like a bear in the woods."

***

Lily sat on her stool at her workstation, her shoulders sagging, staring at her microscope, her hands folded in her lap. She had been like that on and off all day, finding it difficult to concentrate. The necklace was still in her pocket. "It can't be true," she muttered.

"What?" Another biologist passing behind her and stopped, waiting for her to repeat herself.

Lily nervously shook her head, straightening her safety goggles. "Just wrestling a wrinkle with one of my experiments, Billy."

"It'll come to you, Lily. The answers always do." He smiled and kept walking, humming to himself, his paper booties making a *shoop shoop* along the floor.

Lily bit her lip and stood up, stretching her back. "I'll be right back, Claire." She went through the first set of doors, discarding her biohazard suit and booties and getting her purse out of her locker, stepping up to the next set of doors and waiting for the soft whoosh as they opened far enough for her to slip through. She pressed her fingers against the spot where the chip was just under her skin, her chest tightening. She walked with her head down along the familiar path to the ladies' room, only looking up long enough to nod at a coworker headed in the opposite direction.

She got closer to the vents at the southeast corner of the center of the building and smelled a heavy floral perfume. She slowed down trying to place it and realized where she had smelled it before. "Oriceran," she whispered, looking around to see if anyone else had noticed. She glanced up as she passed directly underneath and saw small particles of yellow floating in the air above her. *Vella pollen. That can't be. It's illegal on both worlds.*

Lily ducked into the ladies' room to pull out her phone, looking at her Aunt Lois' number. "What if I'm wrong? The Silver Griffins will come marching in here and there'll be a reasonable explanation and my career will be over. All those years of school and loans." She slid the phone back in her purse and unzipped the inside pocket, looking down at the necklace. The ache grew in her chest. "I need proof."

"Of what?" Fran Shockley came out of a stall adjusting her bra.

"That something actually worked. Sorry," she said, trying to smile, "can't say more than that. You know, clearance."

"Sure, of course," said Fran, stepping up to the sink and holding her hands under the soap dispenser.

Lily pulled her purse close to her chest and walked back out of the bathroom, sliding her wand out and holding it by her side, pushing most of it up her sleeve. She passed back under the cloud of pollen holding her breath, careful not to breathe in the hallucinogen and walked to an empty alcove. She slid out her wand and tapped the chip, redirecting the information it was putting out to read as if she was on her stool in the lab. "Please let me be wrong. I like this job," she muttered, straightening her shoulders and standing up straight. She gave a small jerk to the wand, the end lighting up and whispered just loud enough for the spell to work. "Finders keepers, losers weepers." One of the first spells any witch or wizard learned and was taught to every human child. That way if a young witch was overheard, no one would ever notice.

The wand vibrated in her hand and she slid it back up her sleeve, walking toward the stairs, opening the heavy door and going out to the landing. "Might as well try going up, first," she muttered, looking up the center toward the top. She started up the stairs and felt the wand's vibrations pick up ever so slightly. At the next floor she opened the door and leaned out as the vibration smoothed out. "Not here." She stepped back and gently shut the door, trudging up the next flight as the vibration continued to build.

Two more flights and two more stops at the door before the vibrations finally picked up even further at the tenth floor. Lily stepped out onto the floor and walked to the next turn where the smell of the Vella flower was even stronger. She stopped, listening for any sound of people. She hesitated when she heard nothing. She checked her watch and saw that the cafeteria wouldn't be open yet and there was no town hall meeting.

The yellow pollen floated over her head, seeping out of the labs that she knew were just down the hall. She bit her lip again, working up her courage and was about to turn the corner when the air shimmered next to her and she pressed herself back against the wall, wondering if she should run.

A portal burst open and Correk stepped out, grabbing Lily by both arms, dragging her toward him. He lifted her up into his arms without saying a word, whispering, "Quiet," as he stepped back through, letting the portal close just as quickly. Lily was too afraid to take a breath, much less make a sound as he put her down in the kitchen of the townhouse on N Street.

"You're the Fixer, aren't you?" Lily finally squeaked out. "What just happened?"

"You were walking into a trap, Lily Sharpton and there was no time to spare. Why would Wolfstan Humphrey be after you?"

Lily pressed her lips together but let the wand slide out of her sleeve, putting it down on the kitchen table. She opened her purse and reached into the little pocket, pulling out the necklace with the dried blood and held it out for Correk to see. "I found this in his desk. What does it all mean?" she asked. "I wanted to say something, but I don't know. I needed to be sure."

Correk carefully took the necklace from her hand and saw the royal seal on one side. He held it up by the chain, letting it dangle and turn to reveal the name on the back. "Fraekin." Correk felt a weight lift from his chest and brushed away a tear. He dropped the chain into his other hand and grabbed Lily, hugging her tight. "Thank you," he whispered into her hair, surprised at how much it meant to him.

Wolfstan Humphrey came running down the short hallway, a laugh caught in his throat as he came around the corner and found the space empty. He turned around and looked back the other way, running back to the door at the stairs and looked up and down but saw no one. His eyes glowed as he searched for the magical that had used the child's spell to trace the pollen but there was no sign of anyone.

Things were really not going Wolfstan's way, but he had faced worse, like Trevilsom Prison and still come out on top. It was just going to take a little more effort and a faster timeline, maybe a few more sacrifices by others, but he would get the respect he deserved, or kill everyone trying.

CHAPTER TWENTY-SIX

"I'm tired of waiting." Queen Saria stood at the end of one of the stacks, peering around both sides for a Gnome. "I need a spell, and I want it now."

A Gnome peered around the corner, the poppy on his hat baring its teeth at the queen and growling. "You know we can't do that," said the Gnome, unwilling to come out any further.

The queen crossed her arms over her chest. "Do it or else."

"I'm afraid I'm going to have to go with, or else."

The queen's eyes were hooded, and she arched her brows, the vines on her crown curling and turning black at the tips. "Fine. I have other resources at my disposal. I will call out the guards."

"You promised Correk."

"I promised to give him time," shouted the queen, her voice icy. "Time is up!" She picked up a book, drawing out the gnome who held out his hands in a prayer, pleading.

"No, not that one. It's a delightful little book and one of

a kind." The poppy on his bowler hissed and growled at the queen.

"All of the books in here are one of a kind."

"Then you see my point."

The queen pulled back her hand, ready to throw the book when a portal opened behind her. She whipped around, still clutching it high in the air, surprised to see Correk stepping through with the young, Lily Sharpton. "You are late," she said, evenly, finally lowering the book. The Gnome reached out for the book, making it slip from the queen's grasp and fly through the air to him. She glanced back at the gnome, narrowing her eyes and he ducked back behind the stack, out of sight.

"This had better be good. My patience is running out," said the queen, waiting for the pair to come closer to her.

Lily stayed frozen on the spot where the portal had closed, her mouth open, taking glances at the horses moving in the painting on the wall.

"Why do you keep bringing these uninitiated magicals into the palace, Correk? First Leira Berens, now... Who is this child? A witch?"

"Lily... Lily Sharpton," the witch stuttered.

"Lily has something to tell you that will give you the name of the real killer." Correk put his hand firmly in the square of her back and steadily pushed her forward. "Tell her what you found."

"I am a biologist at Fleeker Corporation on... on the other world." Lily leaned to the right to get a better glimpse of the Gnomes who were peeking around the stacks at her, the poppies all blowing raspberries at her.

The queen shook her head. "I don't need a bio. Give me the name."

"Your majesty, a little forbearance," said Correk. "It will make sense momentarily."

"I was looking for some fliers and it was a simple spell, but instead it took me into a different office. The CEO's office and to a drawer where I found this." Lily opened her hand and held up the necklace with drops of dried blood clinging to it.

The queen's expression changed, and she lifted her chin walking closer to Lily, looking at the name, Fraekin, dangling back and forth. The queen looked Lily up and down and put her hand on the witch's arm, her eyes glowing as she wove a thin stream of magic around the witch. "You're not lying." Queen Saria let go and held out her hand, waiting for Lily to drop the necklace into it. "Give me the name," she said as the cold metal settled in her palm and she closed her fingers around it.

"Wolfstan Humphrey," whispered Lily. "I found it in his desk."

The vines on the queen's crown grew blacker and her chest moved up and down as she breathed faster with anger. "Wolfstan Humphrey, the parasite." Her eyes widened with surprise. "I believe I may have made a deal with that devil. Well, I'm going to correct that and hunt that bastard down." She looked at Correk, not saying anything for a moment, searching for the right words. "I owe you and Harkin an amends. I was wrong. I should not have jumped to conclusions. I'm afraid the past has made me more jaded than I'd like to admit. Tell your father he is welcome back in this world and in this court. Let this be the start of a new day. We have all suffered enough, and Wolfstan Humphrey has not. I will see to it that he does."

Lily sat across from Leira and Correk at their kitchen table in the townhouse on N Street. "You don't have to do this," said Leira. "You probably shouldn't do this. You're not trained for warfare, you're a biologist who just happens to be a witch."

"I loved that job," said Lily, brushing away a tear. "Just days ago, I went to work, proud of what I was doing. Wolfstan Humphrey stole that from me." She held out her hands, moving them as she spoke. "And that's the least of what he's done. He has to be stopped." She took a sip of the warm Dr. Pepper, trying to settle her stomach. "I'm the only one who can walk into Fleeker without raising the alarm. You need me and you know you do."

Leira reached out for her hand and squeezed it. "What do you think, Correk?"

"I think Lily gets to decide for herself. But you realize Wolfstan is playing for keeps. If he finds out, I may not get there in time, again."

"He's the one who got Lacey killed, isn't he? And there's more, I can tell." She shook her head. "I know some of what we've been working on and if there's magic involved, dark magic then this could be really bad. I'm going back and I'm finding out the truth, and then I'm telling everyone."

"I don't think I've ever known anyone braver, Lily," said Leira.

"I'm terrified, but if I don't do this and he hurts more

people… I can't live with that. There has to be magicals in this world who are willing to do the right thing, even when the odds aren't very good."

"Before you go back, we're going to teach you a few things and we're going to set up a way for you to contact me," said Correk. "I can hear you, your magic, without you doing very much at all. I'll know if you need me almost instantaneously."

"We will do our best to keep you safe."

"Will you tell my Aunt Lois for me? I can't bear the look she'll give me, and she'll just try and stop me."

Leira glanced at Correk but nodded. "Sure, we can do that for you. I want you to know you can change your mind at any time. No one will think less of you and we'll find another way to get him. This is not all on you."

"Why don't you think about it overnight? You can take our guest room. It's not renovated yet, but the bed is new," said Correk, smiling, trying to put her at ease.

"I'm not going to change my mind."

"Okay, but in the morning tell us again what you decide, and we'll support you," said Leira, getting up to hug her. "All the way."

Lily sat on the shuttle heading up the curving driveway of Fleeker Corporation, winding past the manicured flowers. Her hands were resting on her purse, her fingers gripping the handles to hide her nerves. *I can do this. I know I can do this.*

Her phone buzzed and she pulled it out, looking down

at the text from her Aunt Lois. *What are you doing? Come home.*

Lily cleared the screen and locked it, sliding it back in her purse. "I will find the truth," she whispered, leaning over to look out the window up at the top floor. "And then I will tell everyone."

The story is far from over. Leira's adventure continues in *RISE OF MAGIC*.

Get sneak peeks, exclusive giveaways, behind the scenes content, and more. PLUS you'll be notified of special **one day only fan pricing** on new releases.

Sign up today to get free stories.

Visit: https://marthacarr.com/read-free-stories/

AUTHOR NOTES - MARTHA CARR
UPDATE: JULY 9, 2020

If you're reading this you know this is an entirely new book. That'll be true of all four of these. They are a continuation of the new stories in books one through eight and it's not one year later – it's just a few weeks. Everything is coming together in these four books in more exciting adventures and a few more laughs. Plus a few favorites popped up that weren't there before.

These books are set in my old hometown of Washington, DC. It's where I grew up a million years ago. (So long ago there was no subway and no beltway yet. Washington was still more of a sleepy town.) I was raised in Alexandria on the grounds of the Virginia Seminary. My late father was a minister in charge of fundraising and the magazine.

I had the run of a large, green space in the middle of a city and a lot of students who didn't mind picking up a softball game at a moment's notice. That's why the Seminary pops up in book eight as a refuge. I think the Dean would have loved to have known he's magical.

Or that bar down by the water in Old Town that served

beer in an enormous glass. It usually was warm before I could get to the bottom. I'll probably put that bar in there somewhere. I'll check and see if it's still open first. The neighborhood has changed a lot.

There will be more places I remember stuffed into these new editions (anyone remember the Exorcist stairs in Georgetown? We used to run up and down them late at night), and lots more plot twists so keep reading. Plenty more adventures to follow.

Then: May 27, 2018: Here we are the dawn of a new age for Leira and Correk and Yumfuck... Whew! It's one year later and the world has already changed. Magic is on the table and things are a little rough. No worries – our team is up to it. Michael and I are working on four series together – Rewriting Justice (Leira 2.0), I Fear No Evil (Shay), The Incredible Mr. Brownstone (Brownstone), The School of Necessary Magic (Alison) and there will be fun and exciting crossovers in all four series. If you've read this far you've already seen some of it. There's more planned!

Also cool because I'm at the beginning of a new adventure. Moving into Austin with a new home being built and selling the first home I ever bought. It's an ongoing opportunity to let go, be grateful, move on, repeat. Two more months, though and the next phase begins. Probably less magic than Leira but also less drama – hopefully a new tribe of regulars...

About the new house... just to keep Anderle honest... (read the next author notes – you'll see) this is my dream house with some pretty sweet upgrades and yes... yes, I do want him to experience the upgrades and in particular

AUTHOR NOTES - MARTHA CARR

touch the master bathroom tile floor. It has *texture.* I've had bathrooms with texture before, but it was from the missing tiles. This is going to be an entirely different experience. Who wouldn't want their fave collaborator to get the chance to enjoy the fabulousness too? I'm generous like that.

As for the future, we'll keep the stories coming – I'll do my thing and bring the magic, bring the thriller and Michael will bring the sci fi and the adventure and we'll come up with more fun. Maybe even a little local chaos… (cackle). And I'll be settling into the new house, getting to know the local music scene better, and creating that tribe. Looking forward to that next chapter… Bring it on!

Ok, for the record, I have *NEVER* run up and down stairs that were in a famous horror movie. Honestly, I'm scratching my head because I think, "Who would want to do something like that? What compels a person..." Oh, **beer**.

Welcome to the new. Martha has put all sorts of intriguing plots and twists in the original eight books for the Leira Chronicles, and now you get to read them and let them all play out. If you are new to this story, then no big deal.

If you are reading book nine without reading books one through eight. I hope you take the time to catch up. Lots of shenanigans (I love that word) have happened you might want to catch up on.

I was talking to Martha last week about a potential upgrade to the new house (which really was new in the old author notes) having to do with her backyard.

Now, I can understand enjoying the updates and upgrades to a backyard, still having problems with the touching of flooring tile – just being honest here. I think Martha and I might be having communication cognitive dissonance over this particular concept.

But, she and I can't have one conversation without "Gotta go" and then five minutes later "No really, this time I gotta go" and finally "Ok, one last item and I have to split."

So, no big surprise, here we are a couple of years later, and we haven't finished this discussion.

In closing I'll mention this little scene in my head:

<Bar, old town, warm beer, fuzzy-eyed college people>

Girl: "I'm almost there," she eyes the bottom. "One more sip, and then what do you want to do?"

Girl2: "We could walk home, try not to be too tipsy."

Girl1: "Sounds boring."

Girl2: "Or we could run up and down the horror ghost-ridden stairs while singing the theme song to *The Exorcist...*"

Girl1: "Right, let's do that." <<Drinks last of tepid beer.>> "Duh da da da..."

Original: May 24, 2018

First, THANK YOU for not only reading Leira's story, but reading through these author notes, as well!

This book is the first in the second series for our heroine, Leira. While I don't want to go too much into the first series (The Leira Chronicles), suffice it to say that her life drastically changes from the opening pages of Waking Magic where she is running down a perp in Austin, Tx. (oblivious about magic) to where she is *now*.

With a light elf and a troll.

Unfortunately, our world has turned rougher since then and in response, Leira is reacting to all of the challenges that she and her friends have been through.

Including her relationship with the government itself.

The challenge (at least from the government's side) is that Leira isn't someone they can just boss around anymore but they need her too much to ignore her. On Leira's side, she has decided she will help, but it won't be free anymore and *constrained* by rules for politic's sake.

She won't allow others to mistreat her by abusing her natural desire to help.

It's a new world and somehow, she has been placed in a pivotal role which helps change the future.

MARTHA CARR

So, I was on the phone this evening with Martha (I'm in Boston, she is in Georgetown near Austin, Tx) and we were talking and catching up since it had been a while. In between laughing (she has a penchant for saying 'clearly' which I typically find funny-as-hell) we spoke about our plans for Leira and Corrick, Yumfuck, James Brownstone, Shay and Allison and where the hell Oriceran is *going*.

I mean, just because we will have probably 44 total books in those four new series out by end of year, there is no reason not to think ahead, am I right?

Well, I was having a moment of concern where I was thinking. 'Do I have any other characters in me than James Brownstone? Am I stuck because he is doing so well? Will I be able to...'

I've had him, Shay and Allison in my brain at some level for a year, and I shared with Martha I wasn't sure I had another set of characters or ideas post Brownstone for Oriceran.

That's when Martha started to scare me.

You see, she comes from Thriller-ville writing and started discussing the political machinations of the large countries and how we would have to adjust this or that, and what societies might implode and it *scared the crap out of me.*

(I didn't want to write that kind of book or even talk about the beats on that stuff.)

In fact, she scared me so bad my mind was running hard to come up with ideas that I felt could work *EVEN* though I've got another 7 books to finish with Brownstone (and therefore time.)

No, in order for me to sleep easier that evening, my mind was working to provide me the barest glimmer of hope I'd come up with something.

While the fan's might continue loving Brownstone enough to extend his series from 12 books to 20 or something, I wasn't entrusting that would be sufficient to mitigate the risk of having to deal with Martha.

Oh no.

No, I needed to come up with ideas RIGHT THEN or risk having to work at the macro level with system governments and I didn't like that idea at all. (I've already done some of that with my Kurtherian Gambit series and frankly I'm not wishing to do it *again* at this time.)

I came up with a few ideas. (EUREKA! – *No, not really.*)

However, I do feel if I need to pack the Brownstone series in at 12 books, I have the very beginning concepts which could be fun for the readers and writers to move forward.

Needless to say, I'm not so sure I'll ever speak to Martha and make the offhand comment, "I might not have ideas for anything past <Enter series I'm working on right now...>" for fear that she will whip out the destruction of mankind's political structures and require me to put them back together again.

<That is WAY too much homework.>

MARTHA'S HOUSE

I received word today from Martha that her present house is under contract to be sold (WOOHOO!) Which means she is about two (2) months from moving into her new house. The problem (at least for me) is the 'touch the upgrades'.

The story...

About a month ago, Martha was enthusiastic and excited about her trip to the designers of the company which is building her home. She was sharing with me on the phone (she lives in Austin, I'm in Las Vegas) how many upgrades she had purchased and how it made her feel.

Then, the *feelz*.

Martha: "That's right, I want you to come over and I'm going to make you touch all of the upgrades."

Mike (a little scared) : "Did I understand you right? You want me to *feel* all of your upgrades?"

Martha: "Yup, I want you to feel all of my upgrades to the house, especially the stone." (in the bathroom I think she said? I forget.)

Either way, she came across so urgently in April that

I'm still talking about freaking out at the End of May. It's feeling a bit like Misery (in my mind.)

It doesn't help my comfort level to hear her cackling about it, either.

I can't tell if she is cackling because she finds it funny that I'm concerned, or that she really cackles with delight

And Now...

The other three series that are 'beyond' this Leira series are The Unbelievable Mr. Brownstone, I Fear No Evil (Shay) and School of Necessary Magic (Allison). Martha and I have worked these four series to work together, and you don't have to finish Leira to enjoy the later books because they are set about twenty (20) years in the future. So, while there will be some cool connections, nothing that happens in this series with Leira is needed to know to enjoy the other stories.

I'd like to say 'thank you' one more time for enjoying our stories. We work hard to provide you fun entertainment and hope that you enjoy as many of our stories across our many LMBPN Publishing Universes. Further, if you are reading a collaboration series, I encourage you to read the personal work of our collaborators as well (you will find their other books in the back of the stories).

Enjoy your week!

Ad Aeternitatem,

Michael

If smart phones and GPS rule the world - why am I hunting a magic compass to save the planet?

Austin Detective Maggie Parker has seen some weird things in her day, but finding a surly gnome rooting through her garage beats all.

Her world is about to be turned upside down in a frantic search for 4 Elementals.

Each one has an artifact that can keep the Earth humming along, but they need her to unite them first.

Unless the forces against her get there first.

AVAILABLE ON AMAZON AND IN KINDLE UNLIMITED!

CONNECT WITH THE AUTHORS

Martha Carr Social
Website:
http://www.marthacarr.com
Facebook:
https://www.facebook.com/groups/MarthaCarrFans/

Michael Anderle Social
Website:
http://www.lmbpn.com
Email List:
http://lmbpn.com/email/
Facebook
https://www.facebook.com/LMBPNPublishing

www.ingramcontent.com/pod-product-compliance
Lightning Source LLC
Chambersburg PA
CBHW050240110726
47898CB00007B/2223